"Why do you keep staring at me whenever I eat?" Laura asked, licking her lips nervously.

"I stare at you when you're eating because your mouth is magnificent. You do things with it that drive me wild," Kyle answered in a husky voice.

Laura flushed. "Oh. I see."

"Do you? Then maybe you can tell me what we're going to do about what's happening between us?"

She didn't bother to deny his statement or to play coy—there was no sense in pretending. "I don't know."

"You're not ready." It was a statement of fact rather than a question, and he was right.

"I'm sorry."

"Don't be. It'll happen eventually. You know that, don't you?"

Laura knew he'd spoken the truth, the truth she'd already acknowledged and known all along, since that moment they had looked at each other seven months ago. What was going to happen between them was inevitable. It was just a matter of when. "Yes, I know..."

Jan Mathews

Although she grew up on a farm in a small southern Illinois town and has lived in Chicago for over twenty-five years, Jan Mathews was born in Kentucky and still calls it home. She is a wife, mother, registered nurse, and writer—sometimes in that order. With a son who has a rock band and two other children who are involved in a variety of activities, she is always busy. If she could have one wish in life it would be forty-eight-hour days. She swears that her family, as well as every volunteer organization known to man, senses that she is a soft touch. She has been active in Scouting, athletic clubs, and in the PTA.

Jan's idea of heaven would be to spend a week in the wilderness—minus poison ivy—camping and backpacking. She would love to raft the Chattooga, see the Grand Canyon on horseback, and watch Monday Night Football without being interrupted.

Other Second Chance at Love books by
Jan Mathews

A FLAME TOO FIERCE #70
SEASON OF DESIRE #141
NO EASY SURRENDER #185
SLIGHTLY SCANDALOUS #226
THIEF OF HEARTS #273
SHADY LADY #306
NAUGHTY AND NICE #343
HANKY-PANKY #371
EVERYBODY'S HERO #405
STRANGER FROM THE PAST #422

Dear Reader:

For March, two award-winning Second Chance at Love authors, Jan Mathews and Jacqueline Topaz, provide, respectively, a searing emotional drama and a lighthearted fairy-tale. Married to a detective herself, Jan has placed both her hero and heroine in the exciting and dangerous world of law enforcement, while Jacqueline unites a veterinarian and a wealthy executive who's not above dressing as Santa Claus or Sherlock Holmes when the situation warrants!

In *Surrender the Dawn* (#434), popular Second Chance at Love author Jan Mathews weaves a dramatic tale of love triumphant. Policewoman Laura Davis will never forget the night she was raped by a mobster. Ever since then, she's wrapped a protective shell around herself, but federal agent Kyle Patterson is determined to help Laura conquer her dark memories. He courts her with romantic sunsets on board his boat, *Sea Witch,* and reintroduces her to life's lighter moments, including a humorous episode involving a "slime monster." Fans of the hit TV series *Cagney and Lacey* and the critically acclaimed film *The Untouchables* will especially enjoy Jan's skillful combination of compelling police drama and stirring romance in *Surrender the Dawn.*

In the tradition of the classic romantic comedy film *The Philadelphia Story,* Jacqueline Topaz expertly blends lightness, laughter, and love in her fifth Second Chance at Love novel, *A Warm December* (#435). Veterinarian Merrie McGregor enjoys the simple life, and has no designs on wealthy, eligible businessman Dave Anders—but, angered by her sister's jibes at her lack of marital prospects, Merrie impulsively claims to be engaged to Dave. To Merrie's surprise, Dave's not only delighted to play along with her charade—he wants to make their betrothal a reality! And with Merrie's five-year-old niece and Dave's dog in Cupid's corner, too, Merrie's reservations must yield to Dave's persuasive charm. With an appealing cast of characters—and animals—*A Warm December* is an entertaining tour de force.

The March Berkley historical romance roster includes beloved Second Chance at Love author Jasmine Craig. We're proud to be publishing Jasmine's first longer work, *The Devil's Envoy*, set in England and the Ottoman Empire. We're also reissuing *Love, Honor, and Betray* by Elizabeth Kary, author of the Second Chance at Love novel *Portrait of a Lady* (#285) and winner of a Waldenbooks Best New Historical Romance Writer Award. For western-romance fans, we're releasing *Silver Flame* by bestselling author Susan Johnson, who received an unprecedented *six* stars from *Affaire de Coeur*, and *Savage Eden* by Cassie Edwards, winner of the 1987 *Romantic Times* Indian Series Lifetime Achievement Award. For readers who enjoy exotic settings and intrigue, we're publishing the first mass-market edition of Theresa Conway's *A Passion for Glory*, set in Revolutionary France and the American South, and reprinting the contemporary romantic-suspense classic *Dangerous Deceptions* by Arabella Seymour. Our Barbara Cartland Camfield novel of love is *Secrets of the Heart*, and our Georgette Heyer Regency reissue is *Venetia*. For mystery buffs, we're offering Edgar Award–nominee Lilian Jackson Braun's *The Cat Who Had 14 Tales*, Ngaio Marsh's *A Man Lay Dead*, and Agatha Christie's *Appointment with Death*. And, finally, we're reissuing another of Agatha Christie's romantic novels written under the pseudonym Mary Westmacott, *A Daughter's a Daughter*.

Until next month, happy reading!

Sincerely,

Hillary Cige

Hillary Cige, Editor
SECOND CHANCE AT LOVE
The Berkley Publishing Group
200 Madison Avenue
New York, NY 10016

SECOND CHANCE AT LOVE™

JAN MATHEWS
SURRENDER THE DAWN

B

BERKLEY BOOKS, NEW YORK

SURRENDER THE DAWN

First edition published March 1988

ISBN: 0-425-10682-9

"Second Chance at Love" and the butterfly emblem are trademarks belonging to Jove Publications, Inc. The name "BERKLEY" and the "B" logo are trademarks belonging to Berkley Publishing Corporation.

Second Chance at Love books are published by
The Berkley Publishing Group
200 Madison Avenue, New York, NY 10016

Printed in the United States of America

10 9 8 7 6 5 4 3 2 1

SURRENDER THE DAWN

PROLOGUE

THE WINDOW SHADES were drawn, and the hotel room was dark and smoke-filled from too many cigarettes. Tension ran high, like a spring coiled too tight and about to snap. Kyle Patterson could feel it as he leaned against the wall, watching and waiting for all hell to break loose. Any moment now, Laura Davis would make the arrest. If everything went well, they would all be credited with the biggest drug bust in the history of the Chicago Police Department.

Only things hadn't been going well the last few minutes—or at least they hadn't been going according to plan. By this time the bust should have gone down, and Tony Calimara, the most powerful mobster in the city, should have been behind bars. Even though Kyle couldn't put his finger on exactly what it was, he knew something was wrong. Perhaps Calimara had outwitted them. Maybe he had grown suspicious and had post-

1

poned the buy. For sure, too much time had elapsed since Laura had gone in.

Apparently agreeing, one of the Metropolitan Drug Enforcement Group officers leaned over the sophisticated recording equipment they had all been listening to, as though by concentrating, he could see into the penthouse apartment across the street and three doors away. "Damn! What the hell's happening? What's the delay?" he snapped nervously. "She's in trouble. Calimara's gonna make her any minute now."

"She's doing fine," the officer in charge, a burly lieutenant named Jim Hines, cut in. "Shut up and listen."

"If he finds out she's a cop, Tony Calimara will kill her," the other man insisted. He was Laura's partner, a young cop who, Kyle had been told, got excited easily. His voice was high-pitched and he gestured frantically. "He'll slit her damned throat."

This time the younger man wasn't being just excitable. There was reason for caution. Tony Calimara was dangerous. The mobster snuffed out life as easily and frequently as he did the imported cigarettes he smoked. Kyle stared at the tape recorder, too. If only he could figure out what was wrong. So far it was only a feeling.

"The wine is excellent." Laura's voice came over the tape recorder then, soft and slightly husky. Naturally husky. She was buying time. Could she feel the tension, too? "Is it a vintage year?"

"Of course," the gangster answered. "Nothing but the best for Tony Calimara. Would you like some more?"

"Perhaps just one more glass. I think I've had my limit."

For the past few days Laura had been walking a

tightrope, "dating" the mobster while keeping him at arm's length, trying to infiltrate his organization on the inside for this particular operation. She was supposed to get close to him, be conveniently present when the goods arrived, and then the rest of the group would go in and make the arrest. It was a simple plan. So simple —until something went wrong.

If something did happen, they were too far away from her to help her, Kyle thought. That was the only part of the operation he hadn't liked. But they'd had no choice. The closest they could get to Calimara without tipping their hand was a small hotel room down the street from his fancy high-rise condominium. Ordinarily there was no hurry in a drug deal. Getting in and making the arrests could be accomplished at an almost leisurely pace, if police work was ever leisurely. But if Laura got into trouble, they were talking a different story.

"Maybe your friends aren't coming." Her voice drifted over the tape recorder again. "It's getting late."

"They'll be along. Are you hungry?" Supposedly the mobster was taking Laura to dinner.

"A bit. Mario's coming, too, isn't he?"

"Mario's bringing my friends. Why?"

"No reason. Just curious."

To the unaware, and also, Kyle hoped, to Tony Calimara, she had sounded fine, but Kyle could detect the anxiety in her tone. He'd only worked with the group for a few days, but he'd been an agent for a long time, and he could tell she had picked up on the undercurrents. *Easy. Go easy,* he told her silently, as though she could hear him. *Don't give him reason to suspect you.*

"Ah, but Laura," the mobster went on, "haven't you heard? Curiosity killed the cat."

She laughed. "But satisfaction brought it back. It's funny, Tony, you don't strike me as the type of man to quote aphorisms."

"What type of man do I strike you?"

Easy, Kyle thought again. *Go easy!* As a Bureau of Alcohol, Tobacco and Firearms agent, Kyle didn't have jurisdiction here, and wasn't in charge, but he had spearheaded the entire operation, and consequently felt responsible for what was going down. According to the information he had received, cocaine was coming in from Colombia and it was supposed to be in Chicago tonight and was being handled by Mario Santini. He had heard about the drug deal on a weapons raid last week in New York, and on orders from the Bureau, he'd immediately flown to Chicago. He wanted to see everything go off smoothly. He sure as hell didn't want to see an undercover policewoman hurt. Particularly not this one. He'd known a lot of women in his thirty-five years, some casually and some intimately, but this one was special—beautiful, smart.

"I'd say dedicated," she answered thoughtfully. "You strike me as a dedicated man."

Good. Laura Davis was an expert undercover cop, Kyle reminded himself, and knew how to handle herself. She'd get out of this one. Or so he hoped. Just before she'd left tonight, she'd glanced at him. Something had passed between them, an acknowledgment of mutual respect, one cop to another, and something else, too. Attraction perhaps, or at least an elemental awareness of each other as man and woman. She was wearing a silk dress in deep red, which contrasted with her long blond hair and creamy complexion. But it was her eyes that had caught him. They were so blue, so innocent, glancing up at him. Innocent, despite the fact that she had to be tough to be a cop. In a way he'd wished he had time to get to know her. But he was assigned to the New York division, and had cases there that needed his attention. And she was a Chicago cop. He'd taken time out for this one strictly on the orders of his chief. Also, she was wearing a ring. He'd noticed it when they met. There wasn't a lot he respected these days, but one thing he did regard was another man's claim on a woman.

"So," Laura spoke again, "do you think maybe Mario got caught in traffic?"

"Perhaps," the gangster answered. "He'll be along in a bit." There was the sound of ice cubes tinkling in a glass. Scotch and water probably. Calimara liked scotch. "You know, Laura, you seem awfully worried about my friends."

"Do I? I'm sorry, I guess I'm just anxious to get going." That was an understatement, perhaps even a play on words. "I'm hungrier than I realized."

"Here I was beginning to think maybe you were attracted to Mario."

Kyle could tell she was surprised by the accusation. Or pretending to be surprised. She'd probably tossed back her long blond hair. "That's silly, Tony. Why would I be attracted to Mario?"

"You're an awfully pretty woman."

"And that makes me fickle?"

"No, but it's been my experience not to trust pretty women." There was a slight pause. Then he said in a low, threatening tone, "Sometimes they're cops."

From the silence Laura was even more surprised.

"Christ!" her partner muttered. "He's playing with her. I tell you he's made her."

"Are you a cop, Laura?"

But she laughed gaily. "Me? A cop? That's ridiculous."

"I hope so," Calimara went on. "Because I hate cops. I'd get awfully angry if I thought you were one."

"Well, you don't have to worry," she answered smoothly. Yes, she was good. Very good. "I'm just a little ol' secretary." They could hear her rise from the sofa and walk across the room. Was she going to the windows to look out? Chicago would be lit up like so many diamonds in the night sky. Kyle had to resist the impulse to go to the windows, too, to communicate with her. *Stay cool, Laura. Go easy.*

"You have a nice view."

"It's only Lake Michigan."

"Which is surprisingly lovely this time of year." She would have turned around and smiled at him. Kyle could imagine her smile: soft and sweet. "It's almost balmy out and it's late fall."

"Yes, we have had nice weather," the mobster answered, setting his drink on the table and walking toward her. His footsteps sank into the carpet; soft, muffled. "But let's get back to our previous discussion, Laura. I'm sorry, but I'm not convinced."

"Convinced? About what?"

"Are you a cop?"

Her tone turned serious. "I told you no."

"So you did." By now Calimara had to be standing close to her. Beside her. "But for some reason, my sweet, I don't believe you."

"Tony, you're so suspicious."

"You're right," he retorted. "I am suspicious. Very suspicious. You see, Laura, I'm not really very dedicated, not in the strict sense of the word, but I am a cautious man."

Suddenly the sound of material ripping split the room.

"That's her dress!" one of the MEG officers shouted. "The crud, he's ripping her dress!"

"Are you a cop, Laura?" Calimara went on angrily. "Are you wired?" The mobster was so well guarded they hadn't been able to plant any listening devices in his apartment. When Laura had gone in earlier, she'd stuck one beneath the coffee table. "Are you trying to set me up?"

"Tony, stop!" *Hang in there, Laura.*

"Good. No wire."

"Of course I'm not wired," she answered. "What's wrong with you? Why are you saying these things?"

Calimara didn't respond to her question. He had started breathing heavily. "You sure are pretty, babe."

"Tony?"

"Real pretty."

Kyle felt a sick feeling hit the pit of his stomach as he realized what the mobster was saying, and how he was saying it. Wrong. *Wrong, wrong, wrong,* his mind screamed. *Get out, Laura. Get out now!*

"Tony?" she murmured, her voice even huskier. She was afraid. Calimara would sense it. Kyle could feel her draw back. "Tony, don't."

"But you're so lovely." Had he touched her, run a finger along her cheek? Rage welled up inside Kyle at the thought of the mobster laying a hand on her. They hadn't considered that possibility. "So lovely."

"Don't," she repeated.

"Don't what, babe?"

"Don't do this."

"Do what? This?" The sound of her dress ripping further echoed through the room. "How about this?"

"No! Stop!" Had he tried to kiss her? Caress her? They could hear her start to struggle. "Tony, stop!"

"Bastard," one of the MEG officers murmured. "Where's her gun?"

"She left it here," her partner answered. "She didn't want him to find it. God!" the man cried, getting up and knocking over a chair. "We've got to help her."

"No!" Hines pushed the other cop back down. "We can't. We're not going to blow this!"

"What the hell—"

"You've been screaming all night long that Calimara would kill Laura if he found out she was a cop," Hines snapped at the other man. "Well, you're right. If we go storming in there like the damned cavalry she won't have a chance."

"We've got to get to her."

"How?" Hines asked.

They were a half block away. Too far away to do anything, and everyone in the room knew it. They all glanced at each other, helpless in this gut-wrenching situation. The sound of glass crashing brought their attention back to the tape recorder. Laura must have thrown something at Calimara.

"Ah," the gangster said, "you've got some spunk. Good. I was hoping you'd be a fighter." So he had planned the delay. That's why the buy was late going down. "We're going to have a good time, babe, you and I. A real good time."

Kyle couldn't stand it any longer. Sickened, he bolted for the door. Even if this wasn't his jurisdiction, he had to do something to help Laura. She was a human being, and she was in trouble. And it was his plan that she had been following. He was about to rush outside when Hines grabbed his elbow and jerked him back. "Where the hell do you think you're going, Patterson?"

It took supreme effort for Kyle to remain calm, not to swing at Jim and fight to get to her. "Can't you hear what's going on in that room?"

"Yeah!" the burly lieutenant answered. "Yeah, I can hear. The question is, can you?"

"I'm going to help her."

"You're not going anywhere, man."

Kyle had seen a lot as an agent, even more when he'd worked on the street as a cop himself, but what was going on in that high-rise apartment was reprehensible to him. Behind them, he could hear sounds of furniture crashing, Laura struggling, and Calimara tossing her to the sofa. "He's raping her."

"I know."

"That's all? You know?"

Hines clenched his jaw tightly, speaking through gritted teeth. "I don't like it any more than you do."

"Then why aren't you doing something about it?"

"Because," he answered softly, almost agonizingly, "I don't want her dead."

"What if Calimara kills her anyhow, when he's done with her? The man's a criminal," Kyle pointed out. "For all we know he might toss her out the window."

"Dammit, don't you understand?" Hines nearly shouted. The veins in his neck stood out in anger. "I don't have a choice!" Suddenly he seemed defeated. "Oh, hell!" Sighing, he let Kyle go and turned away. "This isn't your gig, Patterson. Leave it alone."

"And let him brutalize her?" Kyle was so furious he felt a muscle in his cheek start to twitch.

Hines spun back around. "Look, he'll shoot her.

He'll blow her brains out. I've dealt with Calimara for years, stalked him, watched him, smelled him, wanted him, and he's scum, Patterson. You may have given us this tip, but I know the man. He'll kill her, dammit, and if it comes down to it, I'd rather she stay alive. She's my officer."

"What are you going to do? Just sit here and listen while he rapes her?"

"Yeah." Hines nodded. "Yeah. And I'm going to wait for Mario Santini. And then I'm going to get Calimara, and I'm going to put him away forever."

In the brief stillness that followed their argument, Kyle realized it was too late to help Laura, anyway. Calimara was done with her. They could hear the mobster getting up from the sofa, fastening his belt. Laura moaned softly.

"That's her," someone shouted. "God, she's all right."

A matter of opinion, Kyle thought. He doubted she would ever be *all right*, but at least she was alive. Almost simultaneously, the gangster's doorbell buzzed what must have been a code, several short bursts and a long buzz.

"That's Mario," Calimara said to Laura as casually as though they had been sipping wine all night. "Fix yourself up a bit, babe. There are a couple dresses in the bedroom. Choose any one you want. Maybe you ought to stay in there while I conduct my business deal. Then we'll go for dinner. Oh, by the way, there's a little bauble on the dresser for you. I was hoping you liked diamonds."

"Good God, he trusts her," Hines murmured, almost

to himself. "I can't believe he trusts her. The deal's going down."

"Terrific," Kyle muttered. "Aren't we lucky?"

The lieutenant glanced back at him. "Don't worry, Patterson. I'll get him. Believe me, he'll pay for this."

"He'd better," Kyle answered. "God help you all, he'd better pay dearly."

CHAPTER ONE

THE OLD SONG'S LYRICS were true: It was a long, long time from May to December. Only this was spring. Laura had the months backward. Still, she'd come a long way from that night last fall. Sometimes she thought she was fully recovered. Other times, when she let herself remember Tony Calimara and the way he'd attacked her, she knew seven months wasn't long enough. The rape didn't occupy her mind constantly, like it had at first. There were days she didn't even think about it until she was reminded of it.

Like now.

Across the squad room a young girl sat sobbing and twisting a handkerchief. Another policewoman was consoling her. They were waiting for her parents to arrive. Next would be the hospital: the cold, critical examination for evidence. Then the interrogation, looking through mug shots, trying to identify her attacker, the lineup, the charges. The trial. If there was a trial.

Sighing, Laura turned to her own case, an elderly woman who insisted she had just been visited by Venutians, visitors from Venus, who had told her to take all the wood in the city and bring it to a pick-up point where they would trade her pearls for the wood. Laura had no choice but to arrest the old woman. Stealing, even wood siding from abandoned buildings, was a crime.

"They were tall," the woman explained. "Very tall, and they had beaks and shimmery green feathers. One of them was greasy." She screwed up her forehead in concentration. "Maybe shiny would be a better description, but smooth, you know. The feathers were smooth."

On the other hand, Laura thought as the woman prattled on, seven months as a beat cop was too long. The life of an ordinary policewoman certainly wasn't as uncomplicated as she'd anticipated when she'd transferred out of MEG last fall. Over the months she'd spent in therapy, she'd learned there were as many reactions to rape as there were rape victims, but after the initial shock, she'd done the same thing as many others, which was to try to change her lifestyle. She'd requested a new position and a new precinct, only she hadn't forgotten. She would probably never totally forget.

"What's your name, ma'am?" she interrupted gently. "Do you have a family?"

The woman immediately grew suspicious. She pursed her lips and drew back. "You don't believe me."

"It's not that I don't believe you," Laura explained. "I just need to notify your family."

The desk sergeant passed by, nodding his head toward the old lady and twirling his finger in a circle around his temple. Stooping down, he whispered in Laura's ear, "Loony tunes?"

She shrugged. She didn't like to make those judgments. That was up to a psychiatrist. "Maybe."

"I think Best arrested her last week. She being visited by Martians?"

"Venutians. Where is Ellen? Maybe she knows how I can contact the family."

"Ellen's on a case."

"Figures." Laura sighed again and leaned across the desk. "Look, I'd like to help you, Mrs . . ."

She left the name open-ended, hoping the woman would fill in the blank. But the elderly lady drew further back, indignant. "I'm smarter than that, missy. I'm not going to give my name. Certainly not to you!"

Obviously another tack was required. "Would you like to tell me more about the Venutians, then?"

The lips were still pursed. "I've already told you how they looked."

"Well, you said they wanted you to collect wood," Laura pointed out. "What kind of wood?"

"They *told* me they needed wood to keep warm on Venus," the old woman corrected testily. "They're willing to give me pearls in exchange. Real pearls."

"Right." Laura tapped a pencil against the vase of wildflowers on her desk. Now what?

"They're lovely." The old lady nodded to the flowers.

"Thank you," Laura said. She'd picked them that morning from an empty lot—one of the few empty lots in the city—near the station house. It was a sure sign of summer, softer winds, balmy days.

"I used to raise gardenias."

Laura smiled politely. "Really? They're very fragile, aren't they?"

"Oh, yes. I didn't want them to freeze."

"What?" Laura asked.

"The Venutians."

"Oh. Right." So they were back to that subject. She paused. "Ma'am, isn't Venus close to the sun?"

"So?"

Laura frowned, wondering why she was trying to deal logically with the woman. It was obvious the lady was out of touch with reality. "For some reason I thought it was hot on Venus."

"It is."

"Okay," Laura said slowly. Perhaps she should just give up and book the woman. Maybe she would get an identification through the FBI. Someone had to have fingerprints on file.

"Hey, Laura."

She glanced up as another policewoman approached her desk. Cassie Hudson was a tall, buxom brunette who had befriended Laura when she'd transferred over, when most of her coworkers were uncomfortable speaking to her, not knowing what to say or how to say it. Cassie had been frank, talking about the rape matter-of-factly. In fact, the young officer talked about everything matter-of-factly.

Laura smiled. "Hi, Cassie."

"Pretty flowers."

"They're gardenias," the old lady spoke up.

"Really?" Cassie answered, frowning at the vase of daisies. With a philosophical shrug, she turned to Laura. "Captain wants to see you."

Despite the circumstances, Laura brightened. Perhaps Captain Warner wanted to talk to her about her transfer back into MEG. A few weeks ago she'd put in a request to go back to undercover. Were they giving her another chance? She glanced from the old lady, who was busy examining the flower petals, to the glass-enclosed office of her precinct captain. Strange, she hadn't noticed before that the blinds were drawn. Something was up. And it was more than a transfer.

She turned back to the old lady. "Would you like some coffee?" When the old lady nodded, she motioned for Cassie to follow her to the coffee machine. "Do you know what's going on?"

"No," the other policewoman answered. "But whatever it is, it's big. The head honchos have been powwowing all day. The Chief of Police just left. There's a few guys from MEG—"

"Jim Hines?"

"I didn't catch the names. A big, burly guy. Kinda hairy. I hear it's a federal gig, though, and we're cooperating. There's an agent from ATF, and he's one hell of a looker. Quiet, but one of those strong, silent types built like an Adonis."

The last Alcohol, Tobacco and Firearms agent Laura had met had been Kyle Patterson. And he'd been one hell of a looker. He'd been quiet, too, yet with a seething sensuality. She remembered him as tall and well built with dark hair and piercing gray eyes; knowing eyes. After the rape and Calimara's arrest, he came to visit her in the hospital to talk to her. But she'd turned away from him, too distraught to accept the sympathies of anyone, let alone a stranger.

A stranger who had overheard her violation.

"Do you really think you're ready to go back out there, Laura?" Apparently Cassie had guessed her thoughts. "I know if it were me I couldn't do it."

There were times Laura thought the same thing. Many nights she would dream about Calimara, about not being able to perform undercover, freezing up, blowing an investigation. The fear had become overwhelming and it was something she needed to conquer. "I have to, Cassie."

"Do you think they'll let you? You were pretty strung out there for a while."

"I know." Those in power who decided her fate were naturally cautious. According to all the books she'd read, she'd reacted normally to the rape, but she was a cop. And cops were expected to rise above any situation. It also didn't help that she'd screwed up once when she'd first transferred out of MEG. She'd been working as a beat cop for only a few days, and when the drunk had come on to her, she'd broken down and had been unable to make the arrest. A natural reaction, she told herself. Wasn't she allowed to fail once or twice? But she knew the answer was no, not on the streets. In her job, failure was intolerable. "I've done everything they've asked," she went on, wondering even as she spoke if it would help.

"What's it going to be like seeing the guys in MEG again? Actually facing them? That's got to be tough."

"I'm not certain," Laura answered honestly. That was something she'd thought about, too, and tried to forget. And thought about again and again. Most of the people present that night were her friends, except Kyle Patterson. And for some reason seeing him again was harder for her to consider. But she wouldn't have to see him. Kyle was in New York.

"You were a dynamite undercover cop," Cassie went on. "That should work in your favor."

"Maybe."

"Calimara's still in jail on drug charges, isn't he?"

"Yes."

So was Mario Santini and Tony's "visitors," two big-time dealers from Colombia. Fortunately they would be in jail for a long, long time. But the gangster hadn't been convicted of rape. Laura hadn't even filed charges, not when her lawyer had pointed out that she had every chance of losing and hardly none of winning, simply because she wasn't a virgin. While that type of evidence couldn't be introduced in an Illinois court anymore, all a wily lawyer had to do was make an allusion or two to a jury. It was all so unfair.

"Well, at least the jerk is in for life and hasn't gotten out on a technicality," Cassie said. "Maybe we'll get lucky and somebody will blow him away while he's in the can. Good luck," she went on. "I'll be around if you need me. Why don't we plan on a late lunch after you talk to the captain?"

Laura smiled. "Sounds super."

"Isn't anyone going to help me?" the elderly lady shouted at them across the room. "I'm being ignored and this gardenia is dying. It's freezing to death."

"Sorry, ma'am," Laura apologized. The two women walked back to Laura's desk and she placed the cup of coffee in front of the old woman.

With a smile, Cassie slid into Laura's chair and picked up the case folder. "Oh, Venutians, huh? Say, was one of them tall and green with gold feathers?"

The woman leaned forward. "How did you know?"

How *had* she? Laura hadn't written anything on the file except the single word, Venutians. For a moment she stared at Cassie, too, waiting for an answer.

"That's what they all look like," the other police-woman said, winking at Laura and waving her off.

"Now, where did you say you lived, ma'am?"

Shaking her head, Laura walked away as the elderly woman rattled off her name and address. Crazy. The whole world was crazy. After today, she would be glad to be anywhere in the department but walking a beat.

The yellow twig wreath on the wall heralding spring looked incongruous in Captain Warner's office. So did the half-dead plant buried in the midst of papers and folders decorating his desk. The place was small and musty, but it wasn't crowded with people as Laura had expected. There were only a few men present. Jim Hines sat in a chair. Another MEG officer she'd worked with stood to the side. Suddenly her heart hit the floor and her throat went dry. She had thought about it, tried to prepare for it, but just seeing them brought everything back in vivid detail: the struggle, her helplessness, rage, and guilt.

But she didn't have time to dwell on the past. The precinct captain motioned to a chair. "Have a seat, Laura. I understand you know everyone here."

"How've you been, Laura?" Hines asked, reaching over to shake her hand.

"Fine." She forced herself to smile. "Just fine, Jim. And you?"

"Great."

The captain indicated the other man. "And Stan?"

"Hi." Laura smiled again.

Turning slightly, Captain Warner gestured to someone standing near a file cabinet. "I understand you've met Kyle Patterson, too."

For a moment Laura didn't believe her ears. Kyle Patterson? It certainly wasn't a common name, and Cassie had mentioned ATF. But it couldn't be! Not him! Slowly she turned around. Kyle Patterson was leaning against the wall in the same nonchalant stance he'd used months ago. He was just as she'd remembered: tall, broad shouldered, and handsome, perhaps more so. He was wearing loose-fitting slacks and a shirt with the sleeves rolled up to his elbows, emphasizing the corded muscles of his forearms.

"Laura." He inclined his head politely. Once again she read something in his gaze, something darkly exciting, but frightening, too.

Was she ready for this? To her distress she felt her hands start to tremble. She wasn't prepared for seeing him, for seeing any of them.

"I've got your transfer request here," Captain Warner was saying. "Laura?"

She turned back as he gestured to the group sitting in front of him. "Yes?"

"We've been talking about putting you back on MEG. Think you're ready?"

Until this moment she had been ready. Until this moment she had been looking forward to it; she'd been eager, in fact. Laura stared at her precinct captain, trying to get hold of her emotions. Why was seeing Kyle Patterson so distressful? Why was he here? What did he want? She felt her pulse racing; blood roared in her ears and her stomach lurched.

Laura took a deep breath. She was a fighter. She'd fought Tony Calimara with every ounce of strength she possessed. To no avail. "I . . . I've missed MEG."

"This is a big assignment, Laura," Captain Warner pointed out. "Frankly, I should tell you I'm concerned about your ability to perform." Suddenly he reddened and cleared his throat.

People do that all the time, Laura thought. They stuttered, became embarrassed at the slightest reference to her attack. Suddenly they would stop talking when she came around. Sex became an awkward word. She became known as the officer over at the Lakeview Station who had been raped. Only "raped" had been whispered, murmured in low, disbelieving tones, as though they didn't know how to say it, as though they *couldn't* say it. As though they were to blame.

In all fairness Laura understood their helplessness and frustration. Because she'd been on duty, she hadn't been the only one violated that night. The entire department had suffered. The rape had affected all of them. That was part of the reason she'd requested a transfer. Only now, she needed back in. She needed them to accept her for what she was, a well-qualified policewoman.

"I can do the job," she said quietly.

The captain flushed again and shifted some papers. "Laura, the department psychiatrist thinks you're trying to prove something by requesting this transfer."

"She's right," Laura admitted. Dr. Lowenstein knew her too well. "I am trying to prove something. I'm trying to prove I'm a good undercover cop."

Kyle Patterson walked slowly around the desk until he was looking directly at her. Each step was smooth, fluid, yet slow and deliberate, as was his perusal of her. He stared at her, assessing her. Something prickled at the back of her neck—awareness? Apprehension?

"The street's too dangerous a place to be out there trying to prove something, Laura," he said in his distinctively slow drawl. She'd forgotten about his voice: the low tones, the lazy timbre. "You, of all people, should know that's when mistakes are made."

When people were killed, he actually meant, but he didn't add those words. He didn't have to. They all knew what he was saying. As cops, they all knew their very lives were dependent on one another. And all of a sudden, Laura knew what bothered her about Kyle Patterson overhearing the sordid details of her assault. She'd been attracted to him, and in her mind that attraction had gotten all mixed up with anger and guilt, shame and degradation. Her therapist would be proud of her for that insight.

"I didn't mean it that way," she tried to explain. "I'm not on a vendetta, if that's what you think. I don't intend to kill every criminal I meet. I couldn't. All I want is a chance to show everyone that I've healed, and I'm ready to work."

"Why not vice?" he asked. "Why MEG? Why this particular operation?"

She paused only a moment. "Vice is fine, too, if that's where Captain Warner decides to assign me, but I spent five years with MEG."

"And this particular operation?"

"I put in for a transfer. I didn't know anything about this operation. I don't know why I'm being considered, or even *if* I'm being considered." She paused briefly. "Am I?"

He didn't answer her directly. Instead he said, "What do you know about guns?"

"They go *bang-bang.*"

Now why had she smarted off like that? She knew guns; she could take one apart and put it back together again in her sleep. But that wasn't the point. She was challenging him. For some reason she was furious with him—furious that he would question her training, her motives. Who gave him that right?

Laura clenched her fists in her lap. If she were to admit the truth, she'd say that wasn't the real reason for

her sarcasm. Unfortunately she didn't know the real
reason. But she did know she should apologize to him.
Yet she couldn't. Was she still attracted to him, still
mixing up the anger and guilt? He was a handsome
man, sensuous, tough, and rugged despite the dressy
clothes he wore.

Finally, Kyle asked, "Are you familiar with an Uzi?"

"It's an Israeli-designed nine-millimeter submachine
gun noted for its compact size and reliability," she said
quickly, grateful he had given her another chance. Perhaps now she could prove herself, show that she was
ready to transfer back. "It's capable of firing a clip of up
to forty rounds of ammunition. Cyclic rate of fire is six
hundred revolutions per minute and the muzzle velocity
is four hundred miles per hour."

"Very good." He sat on the edge of the desk, swinging one leg back and forth, his gaze still riveted on her.
Then suddenly he glanced down at her hands. When he
kept staring at them, Laura looked at her fingers, wondering what was wrong with them. At last he went on,
"The Uzi is the latest thing in gang warfare."

Laura was surprised. For sure she'd been on a beat
too long if she had missed that new development.
"What happened to the Saturday Night Special?"

"Not enough firepower. Can't blow away the rival
gang fast enough."

"I gather the Uzi is a problem."

Kyle nodded. "A problem for sure, considering
they're being bought and sold in the United States by
the truckloads. One truckload can cost a million dollars
on the street."

And cost a few million lives, she thought. "Who's
selling them?"

"I don't know," he answered. "I believe it's the mob.

I hear drugs are passé now, and the real money is in gambling and guns."

Would drugs ever be passé? Laura doubted that there was much chance, but it was another thing she could hope for. Drugs caused such destruction. And so did guns. "Where is the mob getting the guns? Where are they coming from?"

"Manufacturers. Also they're stealing them from warehouses. Last month a shipment was stolen right off the deck of a freighter in New York Harbor. And nobody noticed it until three days later when they started unloading."

Laura knew the Uzi was manufactured in Belgium and imported to the United States by only a few companies. She had heard that in addition to the Secret Service, police departments had also started using the deadly weapon. Now gangs. Apparently it was in high demand. "What does a theft in New York have to do with Chicago?"

"A week ago one of the guns showed up in a pawn shop on the West Side of your fair city."

"Any more?"

"Yes, one more, somewhere on the West Side, too, but nothing yet anywhere else, although we've sent the serial numbers out to police departments nationwide."

"Any deaths?"

Kyle nodded again. "As usual, a couple of innocent bystanders."

Laura suspected he was referring to the killing last week of two small children whose older brother—he had been all of six—had found the weapon in an abandoned building and was playing cops and robbers.

"How does MEG figure in?"

"I suspect there are more guns here in the city, warehoused somewhere, and I'd be willing to bet there are going to be more where those came from."

"And you want us to help you find the person behind it?"

"I'd like to shut the pipeline down."

"I see." Laura nodded, knowing already how desperately she wanted this detail. "I can do it," she said firmly.

Kyle didn't answer. He stared at her for the longest moment.

"Look, Kyle, we've never done much weapons work," Hines said. "Like I said before, if this is a complicated plan, you might be better off with vice."

"I prefer MEG," Kyle answered. He glanced back at Laura. "If only because we worked together before."

Although she held her breath in slightly, Laura let the remark pass. She couldn't let every little reference to that night affect her. Even though Kyle had looked at her. Even though they both knew he was remembering.

"Agent Patterson has already explained his plan to me," Captain Warner cut in. "It's got a few rough edges, which need to be ironed out, but I'm convinced your personnel will work best for the job, Jim." Suddenly he paused and glanced at Laura as though just remembering she was in the room. "That's all for now, Officer Davis."

Laura paused. Should she just go? She wasn't normally bold, but she was so desperate to prove herself. "Excuse me, sir, have you made a decision regarding my transfer yet? Will I be part of the operation?"

"I'll be making that decision," Kyle cut in.

Laura turned to him. The sharp tone in his voice took her aback. Was he trying to tell her that he wouldn't be taking her? She'd been turned down for operations be-

fore because she wasn't qualified. It had been that simple. But his rejection—if he was in fact rejecting her—
stung, for he was a stranger. How could he evaluate her
properly when he didn't know her at all? He didn't
know how she would react in any given situation. He
didn't know that her dad had been a cop, that all her
brothers served on the police force, that her oldest
brother had died in the line of duty. And worse, if Kyle
was rejecting her for this detail she was certain it was
because he had been witness to her violation. Like all
the others, he was uncomfortable with the situation.

"When?" she asked.

"I'll let you know by this evening. Will you be
around?"

"I'm off duty at three." She glanced up at the clock
on the wall. That was ten minutes from now.

"I'll give you a call, Laura," Hines said then. "I
know your number."

Laura glanced at the man she'd worked with for so
many years. Did he sound distant, too? Would he be
involved in the choice? At one time he'd respected her
as an undercover police officer. She knew he felt guilty
for not rescuing her that night. They'd all felt guilty.
Would that work for her or against her?

Catching herself, Laura sighed inwardly. She was
growing paranoid. If she was rejected for this operation,
it would be for one reason and one reason alone: They
didn't have confidence in her ability.

"Thanks, Jim," she said, "but that won't be necessary. I'll stick around for a while. I've got some paperwork to catch up on." And a woman who thought
Venutians were visiting.

"Laura," Captain Warner called when she rose to
leave.

She turned back. "Yes?"

"You've got an excellent record."

That was what Cassie had told her. Did that mean he was going to recommend her? Probably not. He'd only been stating a fact. "Thank you, sir."

Laura turned to leave again. Just before she opened the door, she glanced at Kyle Patterson. How she wished she could read his expression, see more than steely gray in the depths of his eyes. What was he thinking, this seemingly passive man who had come into town several months ago with a hot tip and a cool plan?

Unable to tell, she left quickly. She paused a few moments, leaning against the closed door, hoping that she had made a good impression. At last she looked up to face the squad room. As usual the place was a hub of activity. More people were lined up beside desks, being interviewed, fingerprinted, or booked. Or filing a complaint. The police officers present were either typing two-fingered reports or talking on the telephone. Cassie was speaking to a middle-aged couple who, Laura presumed, were related to the elderly woman. The man held the lady's hand and they both hovered over the older woman.

Cassie glanced up, her smile turning to a frown when Laura walked back over to her desk. "Bad news?"

Laura shook her head. "I don't know yet. They're notifying me tonight."

"Missy?" the old woman called loudly to Laura. "Missy, are you coming back to mess things up again?" She was becoming agitated.

"I'm sorry," the man said quickly, both shock and sympathy in his face. "Mama, you mustn't talk to people in that manner."

"Why not? It's the truth. Why, this young lady had

things all messed up. Look, even her gardenia is blooming."

The son looked confused. "Gardenia?"

"Don't worry about the flowers, Mrs. Jenkins," Cassie told her, at the same time reaching behind the desk to squeeze Laura's hand in a gesture of reassurance. "*I'm* going to finish your case." She lowered her voice. "Officer Davis has seen Venutians, too."

"Oh?" The woman looked impressed. "Is that right?"

Laura sighed. She hated leading the woman on, but she had to do it to calm her down. "Yes, ma'am, only the ones who visited me were purple."

"Purple, you say?"

"Some of them are different colors," Cassie added. "Now, why don't you come with me, ma'am? We need to see the judge, and then I thought you could talk to the doctor for a bit."

Laura nodded when Cassie mouthed, "See you later. I'll stop by your place." It was obvious they weren't going for lunch, but that wasn't unusual. They'd skipped dates before. Not wanting to think about what was going on in the room behind her, Laura glanced down at the clutter on her desk, amazed at how paperwork accumulated.

Two hours later she finished filing the stack of case folders. The busy activities of the station house hadn't diminished, and Captain Warner's office was still shuttered. What was going on?

Laura sat at her desk waiting, tapping her pencil against the vase of flowers. It was strange how they looked fresher now than this morning, a feast of beauty amidst the odd assortment of degenerates and deadbeats that tromped through the precinct day after day. She glanced again at the captain's closed door. Then, anxious for something to do, she whirled her chair around to face the detective sitting behind her. "Got any reports you need typed, Ron?"

The man looked stunned. "Loads. You got time?"

"Nothing but."

Smiling gleefully, he handed her a pile of folders. "All yours."

Deciphering his handwriting was difficult, and Laura worked for a long time, all the while keeping an eye on *the* door. After another hour went by she began to wonder what exactly the men inside could be discussing. Not even high-level, long-winded government meetings could go on this long. Then again, she thought, slipping another report in the typewriter, what did she expect from a bunch of high-level, long-winded cops?

Although Laura had been waiting, she was almost startled when the door finally opened and the three men filed out of the office. Her heart started to pound again with a combination of dread and anticipation. She didn't know whether to stand or to sit and wait for them to come to her. The decision was made for her when Hines noticed her, waved and loped down the hallway, away from her. Stan avoided her, too. Only Kyle Patterson walked toward her. The way he moved, so fluid, so wary, so slow and deliberate, made her think he was someone who had not just seen the seamier side of life, but had lived it, experienced it, relished it perhaps, and had survived to tell about it.

He smiled as he approached her desk; a soft, genuine smile, and nodded at the flowers. "They're lovely."

Laura glanced at the daisies. She'd forgotten them. "Thank you."

"Did you pick them?"

Why was he skirting the subject? Streetfighters didn't care about daisies. "Yes."

"Laura," he finally started to say, "I'm sorry we—"

She didn't wait for him to finish. She couldn't bear to hear that they had rejected her. "Excuse me," she interrupted, turning away and pulling a report from the typewriter. At the same moment she whipped around to the detective behind her and tossed the stack of papers on the desk. "Here you go, Ron. I've got to run."

"Laura?" Kyle said.

"Excuse me," she repeated. "I just realized I'm late for an appointment."

"Laura, wait."

Against her better judgment she paused. "Wait for what?"

"You didn't let me finish."

And for good reason, she thought, but he didn't know that. She supposed she owed him an explanation. "Look, I don't blame you for not selecting me for your operation," she said, clutching her purse in order to keep a tight rein on her emotions. "I do understand."

"Laura—"

"No, let me finish. You see, you have to understand, too. You have to understand that I can't just stand here and listen while you break the news to me. I can't hear that you don't want me. This operation means too much to me. I'm a good cop, and yet I'm on trial, and the weird thing is, I didn't do anything wrong. The absolutely unfair thing is, I was the victim."

She paused, getting a grip on her emotions. Then she added, "And the most awful thing is, there's not a damned thing I can do to change it."

CHAPTER TWO

ALL THE WAY HOME Laura refused to think about the fact that Kyle Patterson had rejected her for his weapons operation. She lived on the North Side of the city, near the old Riverview Park. Odd how the amusement park could be closed for years and still be remembered so vividly by everyone, both Chicagoans and non-Chicagoans alike. The site was now the home of a police station, not her precinct, and a shopping center, but the park was still what her neighborhood was noted for, that and the WGN studios. Sometimes she even saw Bozo the Clown, right there on the street.

Laura rented a flat on the second floor in one of the older buildings. A family of five resided below her, a husband, wife, and three little kids, two boys and a girl. Although it was never quiet—until nighttime—she didn't mind. She usually laughed at the antics of the exuberant trio of children. A toy firetruck or balloon was always lying in the vestibule. Once in a while the boys would wait for her and try to fool her with a toy or a trick. They all called her "Occifer Lady-Fwiendly," the last two words run together, like one name.

But today the kids weren't around. As she'd come up the walk, the smell of food wafted from the open windows, and Laura presumed everyone was eating. She unlocked the street door and went up the steps. She left her front door open—as she did most of the time—for ventilation, and started stripping off her dark blue police uniform as she walked through her living room and down the hall into her bedroom.

With a quick motion she wiggled out of her skirt. A shower would feel good. Then she would cook something for dinner. Then she would think about being rejected for the undercover operation.

Quickly she pushed that thought to the back of her mind. One thing she'd learned from the therapists she'd been required to visit was that there was no sense dwelling on the unchangeable. What was past was past. If there was a lesson to be learned from the past, then that was good because the past could then shape the future, but if there wasn't a lesson, harboring on the past shaped the present—badly. And she certainly didn't want a badly shaped present, she thought wryly, slipping off her bra and pantyhose and tossing them onto the bed with her uniform.

She stepped into the shower, relishing the sharp needles of water against her skin. Yet what did psychiatrists know? She respected them, but Laura knew she *needed* to think about the rejection, needed to scream and pound her fist on the wall in frustration or to cry, which was what she really wanted to do. She wanted to sit down and have a good, honest, self-pitying, tearjerker of a cry. She wanted to scream Kyle Patterson's name in rage.

Or Tony Calimara's.

She was tired of being strong, of being the consummate cop. She was a woman, and unfortunately, she was also fallible.

In the end Laura didn't do any of those things, but she was hurt, she finally admitted to herself, and leaning her head against the wall, she let a tear or two roll down her cheek. She hadn't realized herself exactly how much she had depended on getting this assignment. Oh well, she sighed. Straightening, she turned her face to the water, letting it wash over her eyes. She was a survivor. There was always next week. She'd visit the therapist and try again. She'd put through another request, this time to vice.

She got out of the shower and after drying herself, she put on a short dressing robe, wrapped a towel around her head, and wandered into her kitchen. She opened the refrigerator and was shocked by a fierce-looking monster standing on one of the shelves, hunched over and ready to grab her. From the fanged jowls dripped iridescent green slime. Just a glance made Laura feel sick. Ugh. How anyone could actually touch the goo was beyond her. The trio from downstairs must have planted the monster last night, when they'd come up for a short visit. She could almost see Kevin, the youngest, sneaking out with his hand over his mouth, laughing.

Laura closed the door on Attila the Slime-Hun, wishing he would disappear. She'd just opened the pantry door to look for something to eat, when her doorbell rang. Thinking it was Cassie, she went to press the buzzer controlling the bottom door.

"Come on up," she shouted through the intercom. She went to the landing and shouted down the stairs, "I don't have anything to cook for a late lunch but if you've got a good, strong stomach we can share Attila's treasure for din—"

"Hello, Laura," Kyle Patterson said, rounding the final step and appearing at her open doorway. He was still wearing the clothes he'd had on this afternoon and carried a lightweight leather jacket hooked casually over his shoulder with one thumb. Sunglasses sat atop his dark hair. She noticed his eyes were smoky gray, slightly hooded—bedroom eyes. Under ordinary circumstances she would have thought him incredibly sexy.

These were hardly ordinary circumstances, though. What was he doing here? How had he gotten her address? Laura stood staring at him, not knowing what to say. She drew her robe tightly around her, trying to shield her emotions more than her body. The pale pink garment was short, giving a good view of her long, slim legs. The V-neckline dipped low. Yet she wanted to hide the ball of hurt in her abdomen. "What do you want?"

"I think we need to talk."

"Why?"

"I wanted to explain to you about this afternoon."

"What's to explain?" Laura said. Surprise more than anything made her tone harsh. "I'm obviously not qualified for the position."

"We both know there was more to it than that."

"Look, Mr. Patterson—"

"Kyle."

Laura wasn't going to get that familiar. "Look, I

thought I made my position clear this afternoon. I don't see any sense in going over the details."

"I'd like to explain."

"Will an explanation change anything?"

"Not really."

"Then I still don't see the sense." Laura backed into her apartment and started to close her door but Kyle pressed forward.

"What if I told you I'd changed my mind?" he asked.

For a moment Laura was speechless. "What do you mean, changed your mind?" she said slowly.

"I've decided to give you a chance at the operation, after all."

Anger shot through her like a swift bullet. "I don't want your pity, Mr. Patterson."

"Kyle," he answered, "and I'm not doing this out of pity."

She clutched the robe tighter. "For whatever reason, then, I don't want it."

"You don't want to be part of the operation?" he questioned. "Then I suppose you want to keep on booking little old ladies who see Venutians?"

"I want to be chosen for my qualifications, not because you feel sorry for me."

"Look, Laura," he said, "I was wrong this afternoon, and I'm willing to admit it. I've reviewed your qualifications, and I've decided that you're right. You haven't done anything wrong. You were the victim, and we've been treating you unfairly. *I've* been treating you unfairly."

He couldn't have surprised her more if he had told her there were tall green men with beaks on her doorstep. Yet for the second time that day, things didn't make sense to her. Why would he reverse his decision? "I don't understand."

"It's simple. Like everyone else I was . . . am very uncomfortable about what happened to you that night last fall."

That night last fall—interesting way to refer to her rape. And she was as uncomfortable as everyone else, but that wasn't the point. "Then you're doing this because you feel guilty?" That was worse than pity.

"No. I've chosen you because you're qualified."

The word qualified had a nice ring to it. "I don't know what to say," she said truthfully.

"How about thanks?"

She gave a brief shrug, still shocked. "Thank you," she murmured.

He nodded. "You're welcome. We'll be going over the details of the operation tomorrow at my office in the Federal Building. As the captain pointed out this afternoon, we have to iron out some of the bugs. Most everyone is meeting in the morning at seven. Can you make it?"

She still couldn't believe he had changed his mind, that she was actually in on the operation, a weapons raid. "I'll have to check with Captain Warner."

"I've already notified him that you're going to be part of the detail."

"Oh." She gave another shrug. "Then I guess I'll be there."

"Good." He smiled, a genuine smile, as if he meant it.

But Laura felt increasingly uncomfortable. Now what? Why didn't he leave? What was he waiting for? "Who else is involved with the operation?"

"Jim Hines, Stan, and a vice cop named Phyllis Taylor. Do you know her?"

"Not personally. I've heard of her."

"I understand she's an expert at weapons."

"Any ATF agents?"

"Two others, people I've selected. We'll work closely with the branch office here in the city. We can use the central police station for technical support—computer, fingerprints, and the like—but we'll work out of the federal office complex."

"Okay." Laura nodded. That was common in reciprocal operations. State police usually had different technology than federal departments. Together they were able to cover almost anything. "Well, it sounds good. We should make a great team."

"Right." Kyle shifted the jacket he'd been holding to the other shoulder. Was he uncomfortable, too? Equally at a loss for words? "Laura, what happened to your ring?"

She glanced at her hand. "What ring?"

"Your engagement ring. When I was here last fall you were wearing one."

She laughed halfheartedly. Her engagement had been another casualty of that night. "You know how it goes. Cops and marriage don't mix."

"Did you break up?"

Couldn't he take a subtle hint? "Yes."

"You or him?"

"Him, but he was right. We weren't meant for each other." At first she'd been hurt, but she'd gotten over it, particularly when she'd realized she was hurt because of the rejection and not because she was in love. Why was this so important to him?

"I see," Kyle said. "Good. Well, I guess I'll see you in the morning."

"I guess." Why didn't he turn around and leave?

"I was wondering what you were doing tonight," he said abruptly.

"Tonight?" She frowned, and her heart started to beat at a rapid, erratic rhythm. She didn't want to be with a man. "Why?"

"I thought we might go for a cup of coffee." He shrugged. "Sort of get to know each other."

So that was his game! Laura's heart had been right to race. Perhaps she should have protected her body a few moments ago instead of her emotions. She was still standing there in a short, skimpy kimono, giving him full view of her legs, not to mention cleavage. "I'm sorry, Kyle." She used his first name deliberately now, to show him she was in charge. "I'm thrilled to be working with you on the operation, but I'm not interested in anything else."

"I'm offering you a cup of coffee, not 'anything else.'"

Sure. And the earth was flat. She wasn't that stupid. She'd been around the block before. Men pulled that old "get to know you" ploy all the time. "Excuse me, Kyle, who else did you say is in on this operation?"

"Hines, Stan, Phyllis and two ATF agents."

She smiled, crossing her arms smugly over her chest. "Tell me, did you go for coffee with them?"

He smiled, too. "Yes, I did."

Laura stared at him. Talk about stealing her thunder. "Oh."

"You're surprised."

"Yes, I am." Perhaps she'd been a cop too long. She was suspicious to the point of paranoia, thinking every man she met was interested just in a sexual encounter. So many had approached her for that reason and that reason alone. But none lately, none since the rape.

"We'll be working together," he went on to explain. "In order to do that effectively, there's a lot we need to know about each other."

True, particularly when their lives were dependent on that knowledge. But she'd heard that one before, too. Laura stared at him a long moment, trying to decide if he was being truthful. He seemed dead serious.

"So, are you free?"

"Yes," she said. She didn't have much choice. "Yes, I'm free." She stepped back, welcoming him into her apartment. "I'll get dressed."

"Take your time."

When Laura got to her bedroom, she glanced in a mirror and wondered all over again why she hadn't protected her body. She'd been standing in front of Kyle Patterson, whom she had acknowledged several times as a very sexy man, with only a flimsy, short kimono to cover her bare skin. A kimono that did little to hide her figure. With her hair curled in long wisps around her face and down her back, she looked like a wanton woman. And she'd had the nerve to think *he* was on the make!

Quickly she pulled on slacks, and a blouse that buttoned all the way up to her throat, and twisted her hair in the tight knot she wore while on duty. If Dr. Lowenstein had been there, she'd say Laura was trying to put distance between herself and Kyle. She would be right, too. After being raped, that was a normal reaction. But Laura would have done it anyhow. She was naturally wary from all the years she'd worked as a cop. At last, she knew what she was feeling, and that was the important thing.

Laura powdered her nose and applied pale lipstick. Just before she left the room she grabbed a sweater. It was May, but Chicago nights turned cool.

When she went back in the living room, Kyle was studying the pictures on her wall. He glanced at her, staring at her hair and clothing, but he didn't make a remark. He pointed at a photo. "Family?"

"Yes, my father and brothers."

"They're all cops. Chicago?"

"Kansas City."

"You're a country girl?" He seemed surprised.

"Born and bred, although Kansas City isn't exactly country. Cars use the cow trails these days."

Kyle shrugged. "I guess it won't ever live down its Western past."

"Probably not." He was surprisingly easy to talk to, Laura realized. Then again, general questions weren't hard to answer. "Where are you from?"

"New York City by way of Miami and Detroit with a detour through Vietnam."

There had to be a wealth of stories in that answer, she thought as he glanced around her apartment. Big cities with high crime rates, a country at war—what had brought him to all those places? What had he done? Where had he lived?

"You have a nice place, here."

"It's not bad," she agreed, following his gaze. She wasn't very domestic, but she'd sewed the curtains for the windows and the slip covers for the sofa.

"It certainly beats a vagrant hotel uptown," he went on.

"Is that where you're staying?" With drunks and

deadbeats and who knew what else? She stared at him incredulously. The federal government was tightening their budget, but that was ridiculous. They could have at least given him a decent stipend for his trip.

"I didn't realize at the time what I was getting. The place didn't look all that bad, and I needed something right away."

Perhaps "all that bad" depended on your perspective. "A vagrant hotel is something, all right."

He smiled. "It's not the greatest neighborhood. I'll look for an apartment soon."

"An apartment?" She frowned, confused. He was an ATF agent stationed in New York.

"I've been transferred to the Chicago Bureau," he explained. "Since I'm here for good, so to speak, I think I'm going to need something a little more homey than the Wilson Arms." He took her sweater from her hands and held it out for her. "Ready?"

"Yes."

Although he helped her politely with the garment, Laura couldn't help notice that he didn't touch her. Had that been deliberate? Or was she still being paranoid— only now she suspected him of *not* wanting to touch her. Odd, the thought of his hands brushing against her body was erotic, the first erotic thought she'd had since last fall.

"Maybe you could help me look for a place later," he remarked as they went out the door and down the steps. "If you have the time. You know the neighborhoods better than I do. Have you lived in Chicago long?"

"Several years."

"What brought you here from the cattle ranch?" Reaching in front of her, he held open the bottom door, waiting for her to go by.

Laura hesitated a moment, then turned sideways so they wouldn't touch. Did he notice? "Work."

"Police work?"

She didn't get to answer. She tripped over a toy. "Oh!" she cried.

Kyle caught her and held her in his arms. For a moment, as she stood in the protective circle of his strength, she felt fear again—fear of Kyle as a man. Yet something exciting rushed through her, something intense and wildly thrilling. She stared at him for the longest time, not knowing what to say or how to act. Good lord, what was happening to her?

Kyle broke the spell. "Are you all right?"

"Yes." She quickly straightened up, wishing it was just as easy to set straight her confused emotions.

"Occifer Lady-Fwiendly," Danny called, bringing Laura's attention to the child sitting on the floor. "Hi, Occifer Lady-Fwiendly."

Laura smiled. All three children were sitting in the small vestibule rolling a ball back and forth. If she hadn't tripped over a toy, she would have gone headfirst over their legs. "Hi, guys. How are you?"

Danny smiled, gaminlike, and answered for all of them. "Fine. Did you find my surprise yet?"

"What surprise?" Laura pretended she didn't know about the monster.

"Nothin'," he said, but he didn't snicker in anticipation with his brother and sister as Laura had expected. Instead, he looked at her and asked, "Are you goin' out?"

"Yes."

"We can't go out. We're punished," the little girl, Alicia, announced mournfully.

"Mommy's mad," the other little boy added.

"What did you do?" Kyle asked curiously.

"Timmy thought the goldfish was tired," Danny said, pointing to his brother. "It never goes to sleep, so he took it to bed with him."

Laura didn't quite understand why that was so bad. "The bowl?"

"Na, just the fish. It's dead."

Laura tried not to laugh. "Oh," she said. "I see." Kyle was stifling a grin, too.

"Mommy's mad," Timmy repeated.

"Well, maybe you can go out tomorrow."

"I don't think so," Alicia said. "We're punished."

"Fur furever," Timmy added.

Laura smiled sadly. The fish *was* dead. "Well, maybe I'll see you later."

As they walked down the outside steps, Kyle asked, "Would that little trio have anything to do with Attila's treasure?"

So he had heard her shout down the steps. He didn't miss much. "Yes. It was gruesome. They left this monster in my refrigerator that drips horrible green garbage from his mouth. I didn't want to spoil their surprise so I didn't say anything. I'll have to look later when they're around, so they can see how much they've scared me."

"I hear children's toys are revolting these days," he remarked.

"Experts say they're revealing, too," Laura added. "Supposedly a sign of the times."

"I think that theory might be as scary as the toys."

Kyle pointed to a silver Ford Thunderbird down the street, and they walked to it. He opened the car door, and Laura slid inside. She could tell it was a rental. It had that look of not belonging to anyone. Laura was sure there wouldn't be a quarter on the floor or any litter cluttering the car's floor. The glove compartment would be empty, except for official papers.

He went around to his own side. After starting the motor, he said, "Is there a nice restaurant nearby?"

"There are several over on Irving Park Road."

He pulled away from the curb. Since he didn't say anything more she didn't either. Kyle handled the car expertly, weaving into traffic. If he'd driven in New York City, she supposed Chicago would be easy to navigate. Dusk was falling, and he flipped on the lights. "Do you want to listen to the radio?"

His voice startled her. "No, this is fine," she said. "We're almost there." Irving Park Road was just down the block. She indicated a restaurant on the corner. "They have good pie, if you're interested in more than coffee."

"Pie sounds great." He turned into a parking lot, and found an empty parking space. "One thing about Chicago," he remarked, "there's always a chance you'll find a parking spot. In New York nobody drives because there's never any parking spots."

That was something that had always confused Laura. "Then where does all the traffic come from?"

He laughed. "Out-of-towners. Or people who live in New Jersey."

She laughed, too. "Did you like New York?"

He shrugged. "I don't know. I guess so. I don't have any ties so it doesn't really matter where I live."

"No family?"

"Just a sister. She's happily married, though, and lives in California."

The West Coast was a long way away. There was probably a wealth of stories in that revelation, too, Laura was willing to bet. But she didn't pry. Kyle opened her door, and they headed for the café. Again, he was very careful not to touch her, which confused her. She didn't know what to think. On the one hand, she wondered why he was avoiding her. What was wrong with her? On the other, she was grateful he wasn't trying to get her into the nearest bed.

The restaurant was busy, packed with local people having dinner. But they got a booth right away and ordered coffee. Kyle asked for peach pie. Thinking of the treat waiting for her at home in her refrigerator, Laura also ordered a slice.

After the waitress left, she glanced at Kyle. He was busy looking around. She'd noticed he seemed watchful, constantly aware of where he was and what was going on. More so than an ordinary cop. Was it because he was streetwise or was it something he'd learned as an agent? "What's ATF like?"

He turned his gaze to her. "Loaded with red tape."

"That could describe any federal agency."

"Actually, any agency at all."

"How did you become an agent?"

"By accident." He smiled. "I'm supposed to be getting to know *you*, Laura."

"It works both ways."

"I suppose." He paused, as if he were uncomfortable talking about himself. Then he said, "I kind of drifted into my job. When I got back from Vietnam, I decided to settle in Miami, simply because it was warm there. I joined the police force, worked as a detective a few years, and met up with an agent from ATF. The Bureau sounded new, something challenging, not just drugs and sex and murder. Once in a while they even investigated moonshiners. I guess I was ready for a change."

"Is it really different?"

"Not really. It's still drugs and sex and murder, only the cast of characters has changed. Instead of the Miami mob we have the New York mob. Instead of crack it's illegal guns. And you?" he reversed the subject. "What made a country girl become a cop?"

"I'm *not* a country girl," she corrected him again. "And I moved to the big city so I could become a cop."

"Doesn't Kansas City have a police department?"

"Oh, yes. They have a sheriff, too, just like the wild and woolly West."

He smiled. "I don't understand. Why did you move?"

"My father and brothers are all cops. Macho cops," she clarified. "They thought of me as a daughter and a little sister who cooked meals and cleaned house for them."

"No mother?" Their pie and coffee had arrived, and he started eating.

"Oh, yes, I have a mother. But a woman's work is in the home."

He shook his head. "I didn't think there were any of those men left in this world."

"They're a dying breed," Laura answered. "Thank goodness."

"Are you a feminist?"

She considered his question. "I don't know. I'm independent."

"That's a good quality. Tell me, do you have any hobbies?"

She hadn't been asked that question in years, not since she'd filled out the application for the police department. "Aren't you taking this 'getting to know me' awfully seriously?"

"Are your hobbies that embarrassing?"

She laughed. Even when she'd filled out the application she'd hesitated putting down that she collected thimbles. It seemed such a childish thing to do. "Yes. Tell me yours first."

"Sailing."

"As in boats?"

"Uh-huh. I'm docked at Wilson Harbor."

"You're living at a vagrant hotel because you didn't have time to look for an apartment and yet you brought your boat with you from New York?" she asked in disbelief. "Dock space in Chicago is harder to find than the proverbial needle in the haystack."

"I guess that shows you my priorities, doesn't it? Actually, I live on my boat in good weather. I haven't spent much time at the Wilson Arms. Have you ever been sailing?"

"No."

"Would you like to go out on the lake tomorrow after work? It's supposed to be a nice day."

Coffee was one thing; sailing on his boat quite another. Yet Kyle didn't seem in the least interested in her sexually, Laura thought. He hadn't even allowed their fingers to touch when they simultaneously reached for the cream. He was giving her such a wide berth she was beginning to wonder if she had bad breath.

"Yes, I'd like that," she said at last, perhaps because he was giving her so much space.

"Dress warm."

"I thought you said it was supposed to be a nice day."

"It is, but this is May. The lake is still cold, and it's pretty windy out there."

When had he had time to discover all that? "You're staying on your boat now?"

He nodded. "I'll probably spend the summer on it. I guess I'll need to get a car, too."

"Chicagoans do drive."

"I've noticed."

He had finished eating and sat there staring at her for so long that Laura finally said, "Is something wrong?"

He seemed surprised that she had spoken. He must have been deep in thought. About what? "Not really." He picked up his coffee cup. "You have pie crumbs on your mouth."

"Oh." She wiped her lips with a napkin.

He sipped his coffee slowly. Suddenly, he asked, "Are you over the trauma?"

Laura held a forkful of pie halfway to her mouth. He was referring to the rape, of course. She supposed he had to ask and could only hope her hand didn't shake as she placed the uneaten pie carefully on the plate. "Yes, I'm over the trauma."

"You're sure?"

"As sure as I can be without putting myself to the test."

"I suppose that's a fair enough answer," he said after a long moment. "You realize it was an important question for all of us involved in the operation?"

"Yes, I know."

"There'll be inquiries from the group."

She nodded. "I understand."

"And we have to be able to talk about it openly."

This was open? They hadn't even mentioned the word. Yet he was right, she knew. There would be inquiries, and she would have to answer them. She would have to toughen up. "I agree."

"Good." For the next several moments Kyle concentrated on his coffee. Then he checked his watch. "As much as I'd enjoy sitting here talking for several more hours, I really do have to get back. I've got to prepare some papers for tomorrow's meeting."

Despite his streetwise demeanor, he was a sensitive man, Laura thought. She knew he felt her discomfort and was giving her an out. She pushed her plate aside and reached for her purse. "I should get back home, too. Cassie was supposed to come over."

"Who's Cassie?"

"A friend. She'll love Attila."

Although they hadn't stayed long in the restaurant, the hour was late and through a window, Laura saw it was fully dark outside. Neon lights illuminated the street. Kyle paid the bill, and they walked to the car, chitchatting. Once again she was struck by how easy he was to talk to. Yet there were times when he could be so silent. Last fall he'd hardly uttered a single word. His silence could have been because he wasn't in charge and didn't want to step on toes. He could have easily taken over the operation. He was a natural leader. She could sense it. There was something about him that radiated competence. Perhaps it was the slow, deliberate way he approached things.

The ride back to her apartment took only a few minutes. "I'd better walk you to the door," he said, "in case the troops are still sitting in the vestibule to waylay you."

"It's late. The kids should be in bed by now."

But he walked beside her anyway. When they got to the outside door, he held it open for her, like he had before. Ducking under his arm, she went inside. He followed, waiting as she searched her purse for her keys. She unlocked the door and turned to him. "Thanks for the coffee, Kyle. I'm glad we went."

"So am I."

There was something she had to say. "I should also thank you for giving me a chance to prove myself. I appreciate that. And I'm sorry for some of the things I said to you this afternoon."

"*Bang-bang?*"

"*Bang-bang.*"

He smiled. "See you tomorrow."

It was an ordinary statement, so why had it sounded so exciting?

"Yes," she murmured. "Tomorrow."

CHAPTER THREE

CASSIE ARRIVED LESS than a half hour later. Laura pressed the buzzer opening the downstairs door, and the redheaded policewoman breezed up the stairs, chatting all the while. "I tell you, Laura, one of these days I'm going to quit this job and find something dull and boring, like private secretarial work or grocery-store clerking."

Laura went to the apartment door to greet her friend. "I hate to break it to you but those are both busy jobs."

"Then I'll be a blob or something."

"Did you have to stay late?" Laura asked, feeling a bit guilty since Cassie had taken over Laura's case.

"Yes and no. I guess it's a classic example of being in the wrong place at the wrong time. I walked into the station and one of the detectives grabbed me to appear in a lineup."

"What kind of case?"

"Homicide."

"You got off, of course."

"Just barely," Cassie said. "Do you believe it? The broad they arrested is a dead ringer for me, only she's about two inches shorter, ten pounds heavier, and three hair shades lighter. I had to stand next to her and the old man who was an eyewitness has cataracts. He almost fingered me."

"Good thing you lost weight last month," Laura joked and Cassie stuck out her tongue in retort. "How's Mrs. Jenkins?" Laura went on. "Did you get her admitted to the county psychiatric ward?"

"No problem there. She started describing the Venutians to the judge, and he admitted her right away. County Psych. I think her family's working on a transfer to a private hospital, though."

"After three days at County she'll need a private hospital," Laura remarked. She'd seen a lot of people who went there and most of them imagined worse things than Venutians.

"You know it," Cassie agreed. "Say, how'd things go on your end? Did you hear any news on your transfer request?"

Laura smiled. "You'll miss me when I'm gone."

"You got it?" Cassie asked excitedly.

Tossing her head back in a haughty pose, Laura announced, "You are looking at the latest addition to the MEG unit."

Cassie beamed and hugged her. "Way to go, Laura."

"Well, it's not a full-fledged transfer yet," Laura explained, laughing, too. She headed into the kitchen. Her friend followed. "I'm going to have to earn my way into that, but I'm in on an operation. A big operation. Want something to drink?"

"Sure." Cassie pulled out one of the wooden chairs and sat at the kitchen table. "Would the operation you're talking about happen to be the one they were cooking up in Captain Warner's office all day today?"

Laura nodded. "The very one."

"Secret?"

"Kyle didn't say, but I'm assuming that, like most police setups, it's got a lid on it." She got some ice cubes from the freezer and dropped them in glasses.

"Kyle?" Cassie repeated. "Is he the gorgeous hunk from Firewater, Smoke and Arms?"

"I have to be careful I don't slip up and call it that," Laura said, getting a cola from the bottom of the refrigerator. "He might not like my making fun of his agency."

"Nobody says ATF unless they can help it. He's got to know. I'm sure the guy's in on police department jokes." Cassie paused. "Excuse me, Laura, I don't mean to be nosy, but what's that in your fridge?"

Laura turned to stare at the refrigerator for a moment. "Oh." She laughed, remembering Attila, and held the door wide. "Don't you love him?"

"Good grief," Cassie said, screwing her face up in distaste at the slime monster. Green goo still dripped from his mouth onto the rungs. "What is it? Some new therapy from your shrink?"

"It's a surprise from the kids downstairs."

"Close the door," Cassie told her. "I've seen enough. Where are the little imps?"

"In bed, probably."

Cassie glanced at her watch, then became thoughtful. "You know, I wanted to have kids once."

"What happened?"

"Someone told me they grow up. I hear the best part's the first hour."

Laura laughed. "You'd make a good mom."

"Not if that's what they're playing with these days. So, what's the gig? Are you going to have to go undercover?"

"I'm not sure of the details."

"No hard drugs if it's ATF. You won't have to date any slimy dealers like Calimara and sit in on a buy."

"That's one good thing, I suppose."

"Just be careful, Laura. Don't push yourself."

"You sound like Dr. Lowenstein."

"If that's what she's saying, it's not bad advice," Cassie pointed out. "The street can be dangerous."

Laura had heard that one over and over.

"Who's in on the operation?" Cassie went on.

"People from MEG. A couple guys from ATF."

"Did the MEG crew approve your getting the assignment?" Cassie sounded surprised.

"I suppose," Laura answered. "Why?"

The redhead shrugged. "I don't know. Cops can be lousy sometimes, particularly to each other. I heard Stan didn't want you on the detail. He thought you might freeze up."

Laura shrugged. "Kyle didn't mention anything."

"What's he like?"

"Kyle?" Laura thought for a moment. "He seems nice."

Cassie lifted her eyebrows. "Odd way to describe a cop. I've met a lot of them and not a single one is *nice*. Does he know about the rape?"

Sometimes her friend was too outspoken, Laura thought. She paused. "Yes."

"What'd he say?"

"We didn't talk about it."

"Why not?"

"Rape isn't an easy subject to discuss, Cassie," she retorted testily. "Oh, by the way, I was brutalized the other night, do you have any remarks you'd like to make about it?"

"Yeah. The guy's scum. Somebody should emasculate the son-of-a-bitch."

Laura laughed. "You're big on revenge, Cassie. I'd hate to meet you in a dark alley after double-crossing you."

"Damn right." Cassie laughed, too. Then she said, "He's awfully good-looking."

Laura frowned, not quite following the logic. "Kyle?"

"No, Attila," Cassie replied sarcastically.

"What does his being good-looking have to do with anything?"

"Well, did you at least *notice* that he's good-looking?"

"Yes."

"You're kidding." Cassie stared at Laura in disbelief. "You noticed? You really looked?"

"It was hard *not* to notice. I do have eyes," Laura pointed out. "Tony Calimara raped me, Cassie, but he left my vision intact." It wasn't often she could joke about the incident. Tonight, however, it seemed far away and almost forgotten. If it could ever be forgotten.

"From what I heard, you didn't notice guys even before you were raped."

"You hear a lot."

"What else is there to do when a person deals with criminals all day long? Talking about the crime rate is too depressing. Have you ever worked in a hospital? I was a nurse's aide once and now *there's* a grapevine. So, is it true?" she asked without skipping a beat. "Do you really disdain the entire male species?"

"I guess growing up with men has made me immune to their charms," Laura explained. "After living with six gorgeous-looking brothers for seventeen years, a man has to be pretty devastating to catch my eye."

"Kyle Patterson's devastating, all right," Cassie said, sipping her cola. "He's got a body that won't quit. I almost envy you working with him on the operation. Now, what's he really like? Aside from being nice, that is."

"I don't know."

"Aren't you kind of excited?"

"Yes," Laura admitted. "I am excited, but I'm sure it's from being back on a detail."

"Nothing to do with the man?"

Laura paused. She was supposed to be honest with herself. Dr. Lowenstein wanted her to admit her feelings. At last she said, "He kind of scares me."

"The man or the thought of sex with the man?"

"Both."

Cassie nodded. "I guess it would be tough thinking of a guy in a sexual way after you'd been assaulted."

"For a long time I didn't think of sex at all without shuddering." Laura thought for another moment. "But according to the experts most rapes aren't sexual in nature. They're an expression of power, a conscious process of intimidation or aggression."

"What the hell good does it do to know all that?"

"I don't know." Laura shrugged. "Truthfully, though, I think Kyle Patterson would have scared me even if I hadn't had a bad experience. He's kind of . . . I don't know, kind of—"

"Fascinating?"

"Yes. And maybe even mysterious, if that makes any sense. There's something about him that's alluring. There's a depth to him that I can't figure out."

"I think you're attracted to this guy, Laura," Cassie said, and before Laura could answer she went on. "I'm starving to death. Would you be interested in going out for dinner? We could get pizza."

"I think I'll pass if you don't mind," Laura said. "I had a piece of pie earlier, and I'm not really hungry. I have to be downtown for briefing at the crack of dawn, so I thought I'd try to get some sleep."

Cassie sighed and stood up. "I guess I'm stuck with bologna and asparagus."

"Is that all you've got at home?"

"Hey, not all of us are lucky enough to open the refrigerator and find slime, but actually I have weird eating habits. I *like* bologna and asparagus."

Laura laughed and followed her friend to the door.

"Talk to you tomorrow. Hang in there and congratulations on your new assignment," Cassie said as she went down the stairs.

And then Laura did what she wasn't supposed to do: She refused to think about anything at all, and Kyle Patterson in particular. The man had given her a chance, and she was grateful for it. Now she was going to sleep so she could be alert at the briefing in the morning.

The Federal Building where Laura was supposed to meet everyone was actually two buildings across the street from each other in the downtown area of Chicago. Everything relating to the federal government, from the FBI to the EPA and the Internal Revenue Service, was housed there. They were all listed on the board in the lobby.

Since this was to be a briefing, Laura was wearing slacks and a blouse instead of her uniform, and she had to show her badge to the guard in the lobby. When she got off the elevator where the security guard had instructed her to stop, she was surprised to discover that the Bureau of Alcohol, Tobacco and Firearms didn't even resemble a law enforcement agency. It looked more like a secretarial pool at a large corporation. There were rows and rows of desks, and here and there sat a fan. Since the hour was so early, the place was empty.

Laura found Kyle, along with everyone else picked for the operation, in a large, darkened briefing room off to one side. Jim, Stan, and Phyllis were all talking.

Kyle nodded to her as she entered. "Good morning."

She nodded back, greeting everyone else with a polite smile. He was ready to begin, she noticed, and he wasted no time. After tossing out introductions, he walked to the blackboard in front of the room.

"The first thing we need to do," he said, writing out names and places, "is to discuss the details of the operation." He turned to them. "What I have in mind is fairly simple. We're going to buy some guns. Naturally we're going to have to put the word out on the street that we're interested in weapons. I figure we ought to start on the West Side, near where the Uzis were found."

"I know a hooker we can talk to," Jim volunteered. "She's one of my regular contacts. I hear her pimp carries a grizzly. He might have heard something about the machine guns and who has them."

"Why the hell is a pimp carrying a forty-five magnum automatic?" Phyllis cut in. "Does he want to blow a plane from the sky?"

"Why the hell does anyone carry a grizzly?" Stan answered. "He likes big guns."

Although she'd never seen the weapon they were discussing, Laura had heard that the firepower of the gun was phenomenal. In its own way it was as deadly as the Uzi. What it lacked in rapid firepower it made up in sheer destruction.

"That's good, but I'd rather we don't use usual contacts, Jim," Kyle said. "I don't want the word out that cops are looking. I want the word out that a bunch of revolutionaries are looking."

"Revolutionaries?" Phyllis repeated incredulously. "We're going to pretend to be revolutionaries?"

Kyle nodded. "If whoever's running this deal thinks a cause is buying, they're likely to try to make a big sale, and maybe we can get the head honcho."

"Sounds great," she answered, "but aren't we the wrong ethnic group?"

Kyle laughed. "You need to develop an open mind, Phyllis. There are more people plotting to overthrow their governments than just South American or Middle Eastern revolutionaries, or even the Irish. We're going to pretend to be from Canada." Nodding to one of the men he'd introduced earlier he said, "Our identification papers are already in the works, thanks to Sam, here, who should be a master forger instead of an agent. I figure we ought to be unhappy with the Canadian government and have a plan to bomb some government buildings and take hostages. We've come here looking for weapons because we've heard the shopping's good and the price is right."

"Can't we get arrested for that?"

"Sure." Kyle nodded. "If we get caught."

Phyllis let out a low whistle. "We're going undercover that deep?"

"Yes. Any other questions?" Kyle glanced around the

room. No one said anything more so he went on. "We've had a telephone installed in this room, and Scott will monitor it. If anybody asks, this will be the number we give. All calls will be traced instantly. In the event that someone does contact us, Scott will notify me immediately. I'll have a beeper."

Stan leaned forward. "And then?"

"And then I'll call each of you. When we go, we go together."

"If we go."

Kyle nodded. "We have to hope they contact us."

"They will," Stan remarked. He looked directly at Laura and added, "This is a dangerous operation."

"Yes, it is," Kyle acknowledged. "When we hit the street we go by pairs," he went on as if totally undisturbed by the suggestion of danger. "Phyllis will hook up with Sam. Stan and Jim stay together. That leaves Laura and me. Is that all right with everyone?"

Laura frowned. Had he planned it that way? And if he did, why? To show his faith in her? He seemed so casual about the assignments she couldn't tell.

"My ex-husband's name was Sam," Phyllis remarked, grinning at the balding man sitting beside Kyle at the table. "Can I call you Sammy?"

"You can call me anything," he answered, "as long as you know what you're doing on the street."

"She does," Kyle vouched. "Stan?"

"Fine by me."

"Laura?"

"Great," she answered.

"Good. We let it be known, though, that there are a lot of us. If necessary, we'll find a building and set up a headquarters."

"Won't someone get suspicious when we ask about

Uzis," Laura spoke up at last. "What about the coincidence of the guns being stolen and us wanting them?"

"We aren't going to inquire about Uzis," Kyle explained. "As far as our contacts are concerned, we're simply looking for firepower. The Uzis are out there. Lots of them. I'm hoping that greed will make whoever is behind this to try to unload the guns on us."

It was a good plan, Laura thought, yet as Jim had pointed out, it was iffy. But not many undercover operations were watertight. She had taken lots of chances before, and she was more than willing to take a chance now.

"Okay." Walking back to the front of the room, Kyle flipped on a projector. "Now we need to know our product. Some of you may already be familiar with this information, but for the benefit of us all, we need to go over some specifications. By the time you leave here, you'll all be experts."

He wasn't joking. For the next several hours they watched films of Uzis, from the manufacture of the gun, even the metal selection, to the distribution of the weapon, including the names of importers. When the movies were over, he distributed folders. Inside were more pictures of the weapon. Next he circulated details of the theft. Then more documentation. Projected firepower. Ammunition. Leftist groups. Gangs. Statistics on organized crime.

Sandwiches were delivered for lunch. Still Kyle didn't stop for a break. By the time lunch was finished, Laura had seen so many photographs and heard so much technical data her brain felt numb.

Phyllis was supposed to be the weapons expert but Kyle knew the gun inside and out, and he inundated them with information, pacing the room as he spoke, explaining, clarifying, instructing. Finally he paused. "Any questions?"

Someone laughed. Kyle just smiled. "Tired?"

"If we admit to it, will you show us more movies?" Phyllis asked. "Or are we done for the day?"

"Your life might just depend on those movies," Kyle said, "but yes, we're almost done for the day. I've made arrangements with Captain Warner for a demonstration firing of the Uzi in the morning," he finished up. "I'd like for each of you to qualify with your street weapon at that time, just in case you've gotten rusty."

Jim Hines raised his hand and asked something about ammunition. During the discussion that followed Laura sat quietly, watching Kyle move back and forth across the room, thinking of his ease of command, and the years it had taken to acquire such knowledge. What had he been like as a cop on the street? As a rookie? Had he moved up through the ranks? He'd worked in Miami. From the little he'd mentioned, it had sounded as if he'd become hardened, disillusioned by the things he'd seen. Certainly something drove him, made him spend hours in a smoky room discussing a plan that might or might not work.

He crossed in front of her. Where was his gun? she wondered, still watching, studying him. Yesterday he'd worn a holster that fit over his shoulders. He'd had his jacket off in Captain Warner's office, and she'd noticed the rig. She'd noticed his arms, too, the hardened flesh, the sinewy muscles. Today he was wearing another jacket along with loose-fitting slacks. She couldn't see the telltale bulge. As he sat on the edge of a table, swinging his leg back and forth, her gaze almost automatically slipped lower.

"Laura?" he said after a few moments. "Is something wrong?"

She glanced up and realized that everyone was staring at her. She felt herself turn red. "No, nothing's wrong."

"Are you sure? You seemed kind of intense. If you have any concerns, please feel free to speak up."

"I . . . uh, I was thinking of something else," she murmured. She couldn't help blushing. He was right. She had been intense. She'd been intensely staring and not at the gun he carried! Cassie would die laughing, Laura thought, and so would Dr. Lowenstein.

"This is a real breakthrough," the doctor would probably say. "You say you were ogling a man's crotch?"

Laura was thankful Kyle stood up and moved from the table. "Okay, that's it, unless any of you have something you'd like to add."

Jim Hines asked another question. Laura sat up straight, forcing herself to pay attention. She kept her eyes riveted to Kyle's face. How could she have done such a thing, have had such thoughts? She had to get hold of herself. Even before the rape she wouldn't have stared at a man like that.

"Well, it's late," Kyle said in conclusion. "After we qualify at the firing range in the morning, we'll hit the streets for a while. See what we can dig up. See you all then. Have a good evening."

Laura gathered all the papers she'd collected during the briefing and started for the door. Stan was talking to Kyle at the front of the room, but Kyle called to her as she was leaving. "Laura? Excuse me a minute, Stan." He walked toward her. "You weren't leaving, were you?"

"I thought we were finished."

"We are. Did you drive here this morning?"

She frowned, wondering what he was getting at. "No, I took the El down."

"If you'll give me another second or so, I'll be done here. I just have a couple more questions to answer and some papers to clear away. I'll give you a lift home, and you can get your sweater."

She stared at him blankly. "My sweater?"

"Weren't we going sailing?"

"Oh," she said. She'd totally forgotten. "Oh, that's right." She frowned again and glanced at her watch. "It's really late."

"We'll be just in time for sunset. It's really a pretty sight from the boat. And I picked up a newspaper this morning. I thought you might help me select some apartments."

Laura didn't know what to say. It wasn't safe being with Kyle Patterson. He made her have such . . . unusual thoughts.

"I don't want to make the same kind of faux pas I did last night, so I know you aren't offering anything except an evening on the lake and a glance at a newspaper, but do you really think it's a good idea for us to see each other on a personal basis?" she asked. "We're going to be partners on an operation."

"Which, as I pointed out last night, is exactly the reason we *should* see each other on a personal basis," he countered. "We can go over our cover together. That way we won't waste valuable meeting time learning each other's little quirks. You know, you never did tell me your hobbies."

"What kind of little quirks are you talking about?"

He shrugged. "I don't know. Silly stuff, like I have a thing about popcorn. Or mints. And serious stuff, like I always walk down the right side of the street."

She smiled at him. "Always?"

"Guess it sounds kind of weird. Actually, it helps if I have to draw my weapon. I keep my gun on the left."

Laura felt herself flush.

"Something wrong?"

"No." She wanted to die of embarrassment, but she knew that even if he'd realized where she'd been looking earlier, there was no way he could have been reading her mind. "In a shoulder holster?"

"Today I'm using a belt holster," he said. "I knew we were going to be inside. And you?"

"I quick-draw from my Louis Vuitton."

"What's that?"

"A purse."

He laughed. "See? We both have a lot to learn. So what do you say? Want to go sailing?"

She thought of the train that would take her home, how it would be packed with people. And they did have to discuss how they would handle their cover. "Sure," she answered. And all of a sudden she did want to go. All of a sudden she wanted him to know her quirks. She wanted him to know that she got up on the left and went to bed on the right, that she drank pop in the morning and milk at night, and that she liked his style. And that despite having been raped, she found him very sensually exciting.

CHAPTER FOUR

KYLE WAS STILL RENTING the silver Ford Thunderbird. In order to save time, they decided to skip going to Laura's apartment. They didn't want to miss sunset on the boat, so Kyle offered to lend Laura one of his sweaters. Traffic exiting the Chicago Loop was heavy, and they drove along Lake Shore Drive with hundreds of other cars crossing the S curve and rounding Oak Street Beach. In the distance Lake Michigan seemed so serene. The water was pale blue with tiny whitecaps whipped up by a gentle wind. The park that stretched between the road and the water was filled with leafy trees and blooming flowers. People were throwing Frisbees or tossing balls to each other and to their dogs.

"You were very thorough at the meeting," Laura remarked.

"And you were very attentive," he countered.

She shot him a sidelong glance, but he seemed serious. Perhaps he hadn't noticed her mind wandering. "Do you think we have a chance to catch whoever is behind the theft of the guns?"

"I wouldn't waste our time if I didn't think we had a chance. Why do you ask?"

She shrugged. "Sometimes it seems like so little is contingent on us and so much is contingent on the criminal element."

"The old needle in the haystack?"

"Something like that."

"I guess police work, even Bureau work, can seem fruitless at times. It sure as hell is frustrating. But there's the other side of the coin, too, when we plan an operation and make a big arrest."

"True."

Switching from the center lane, Kyle headed the car toward the exit at Wilson Avenue. "The trick is to not let the criminals get you down, Laura."

She glanced at him. "How long did it take you to learn that?"

"How did you know I'd let it happen?"

"Some things you mentioned yesterday about switching to the Bureau," she answered as he headed up the ramp. "You sounded as though you'd burned out at one time."

"I did. Between Vietnam and the police department, I witnessed a lot of atrocities, a lot of greed, and a lot of graft." Turning right, he pulled the car onto the road leading to the harbor. "But I think we all burn out at one time or another. What's brought on your doubts? You seem awfully uncertain all of a sudden."

Laura leaned her head back against the seat and stared out the window. Perhaps she'd been uncertain all along, and just fooling herself and everyone else. "I don't know. I understand Stan is unhappy with me on the operation."

"Stan isn't in charge."

"Maybe he's right. Maybe I'm not ready."

Kyle frowned at her as he pulled the car into a parking space. "This operation is crucial, Laura, but it isn't the end of the world. You don't have to flagellate yourself to prove your worth."

"Is that what I'm doing?"

"You're having moments of doubt."

"What's wrong with moments of doubt? All cops have them. Or they should."

He shut off the engine and sat quietly, thinking. "That's true, all cops do have moments of doubt, and there's nothing wrong with that. Doubt is good. It keeps us sharp. But you're assuming a burden of guilt for something you haven't done yet. And that's silly." He reached into the backseat for his suit jacket, got out his side, and went to open her door. "Ready? The sunset awaits."

Apparently the subject was closed. But Laura was glad to know that he believed in her. She swung out of the car and walked beside him through the trees toward the docks. The harbor was crowded with boats. Everything from tall-masted sailboats to huge luxury yachts bobbed gently, riding the swells created by wind and weather. Out on the lake more boats dotted the horizon, looking like tiny white spots in the gathering dusk.

Several people waved to Kyle as they walked along the pier. "I see you've met your neighbors," Laura remarked.

"Yes, I have." He smiled and waved to more people as they went on. "It's a different world down here. Everybody's friendly. The guy you'd meet on the street and ignore in any other circumstances is a good old Joe on the docks. You don't have to be paranoid. You don't have to worry about theft. You don't have to lock up. We're all sailors, and we're all in this together."

"Sounds kind of nice," she said. Particularly when you worked with criminals all day long.

"It is."

They walked past several more yachts. When Kyle got to a long, sleek boat that rode high in the water, he grabbed a rope and pulled the craft closer to the row of sandbags that lined the pier and secured it tightly. "Well, here's home."

Laura didn't know anything about boats, but she estimated this one to be about thirty feet long. It was single masted, had gold railings, and was painted black, with double gold stripes. The sails were down, neatly tied, and all the metal gleamed, obviously highly polished. She noticed *Water Witch* painted in gold block letters on the back.

Still holding the boat close to the dock, Kyle hopped through a break in the railings onto the well-varnished deck and held out his hand for Laura. "Welcome aboard."

She took his hand and jumped across the narrow channel of water onto the deck beside him. The boat bobbed, and it took her a few moments to get her balance.

"Careful," he said.

Kyle dropped her hand quickly, and Laura wondered if it was because he didn't want to touch her. He led her to a padded bench on one side of the boat. She was grateful for the seat and glanced around. Up close the rails were shinier than they'd seemed from shore, and the boat seemed bigger somehow. The black color had been used throughout, even the inside walls. Everything was neat and tidy. Ropes were coiled tightly on the deck. Round life preservers hung in strategic places. A small door in the middle led to what was obviously a cabin.

"It's beautiful."

"She," he corrected. "Boats are of the female persuasion."

Laura smiled. "I'd make a remark about that, but I doubt it would do much good."

"Sailors do tend to ignore claims of chauvinism," he agreed, bending over to move a rope from under her feet. "Yet boats *are* female, and I'd make a remark, too, but you'd probably be offended." He gestured front and back, left and right. "Fore and aft, port and starboard, and no, I'm not docked on the port side."

"Is that a frequent question?"

"With no logical answer."

"This question probably has no logical answer, either," she said, "but why *Water Witch*?"

"At the risk of sounding off my rocker, I'll answer: Sorcery. Magic."

"This is a boat."

"She's not just a boat, Laura," he said, standing up. "She's my boat, and believe it or not, she's a bit magical. She weaves spells."

Laura laughed. "That sounds ominous. What kind of spells?"

"You'll see," he answered, but he laughed, too. "Come on, I'll show you around."

Below deck, things were just as neat as above. The tiny kitchen—or galley, as Kyle corrected—was spotless and cheery. As though it were a very unique feature, he explained that the stove was weighted, and floated up and down, consequently staying level no matter what position the boat was in. If someone wanted to cook, they could do it while under full sail, even when the boat leaned to one side or the other. Laura was properly impressed. Since it wasn't weighted, a thick, stubby candle sat lashed to the middle of a built-in table. His bunk, which seemed very wide, was tightly made up, and his clothes fit nicely into a wardrobe along the wall. Everything was compact, organized.

After she'd put on one of his sweaters they went back up the steps to the deck. "If we don't get out on the lake soon, we're going to miss the sunset," he said, moving fore and aft to toss the ropes that held them in port to the pier. He headed toward the wheel and turned a key to start the engines.

"You have a motor? I'm surprised."

"Why?"

"Isn't that cheating? I thought this was a sailboat."

"I'm a purist, but I'm not that much of a purist," he explained, handing her an orange life jacket. "It's hard to get out of the harbor without engines. And they're damned handy when you're stuck on the water and there's no wind." He gestured to the life vest. "Put that on."

She put on the heavy garment. "Can you handle the boat without a crew?"

Kyle nodded. "It's a big enough craft that I don't feel cramped, yet small enough for one person to sail."

"You don't have a vest on."

"I'm an old hand at this so I'm exempt."

He expertly navigated out of his berth and around the other boats. After they got beyond the breakwater, he cut the engine and unfurled the sails. "Ready?"

Laura nodded. "Sure."

For a moment nothing happened. Then the wind caught the giant piece of canvas, and the boat started to skim forward. Either he had been traveling slowly with the engines or the wind was suddenly wild, because within moments, they were moving through the water faster than Laura thought possible.

"Hold on," Kyle called as the boat cut a swath through the waves. He seemed to be thoroughly enjoying himself. He laughed as the boat leaned to one side, dangerously close to toppling into the water, and fiddled with some lines as the lake sprayed into his face. Laura must have turned green or something because all of a sudden he righted the boat, whipped down the sails, and secured them. He turned to her with a concerned frown. "Are you all right?"

"Just surprised," she answered, still holding with all her might onto the bench where she'd been sitting. The boat bobbed up and down, but at least it wasn't moving forward. "Thank you for stopping."

"Sorry. I sometimes forget people aren't accustomed to sailing."

"This is sailing? It feels more like torture."

He laughed. "She's fast."

"Yes," Laura agreed, "she certainly is. Can I let go now?" Her fingers hurt from the pressure of holding on.

Kyle laughed again. "You can even stand up."

"I don't think I'd go that far." She took a deep, calming breath. "Will we be all right? Don't we have to put down the anchor?"

"We'll be fine. We'll drift a bit. The anchor's just for staying stationery if you aren't going to be around to supervise."

"You will supervise?"

He shook his head in disbelief. "I think you're a

landlubber, Laura Davis, but yes, I will supervise. Did you want to see the sunset? Turn around. We're just in time."

Although Laura clung to the seat, she turned and was awed by the sight. The sun was half buried in the horizon, big and round and red. Red, gold, and yellow rays streaked through the clouds, staining everything around with brilliant hues of color. It seemed as though the waves were lapping against the flaming sun, right up against the blaze. With the fine mist of fog that barely shrouded the water, she could almost see steam.

"Beautiful, isn't it?"

Laura could only stare. "Gorgeous. Where's the shoreline?"

"We're out just far enough that we've lost it." He gestured to one side. "It'll come back in sight as we get closer. You can see the buildings downtown, though, since they're on a different angle."

The Chicago skyline was almost as lovely as the sunset. Spires of tall buildings reached for the sky, and as the boat bobbed, they seemed to dip and rise. Laura felt as if she were on a roller coaster ride. She watched as the ball of fire disappeared and lights began to twinkle from the city. The wind blew through her hair and she shivered.

"Cold?" Kyle asked. "I can get you a coat."

She wrapped her arms around her, not wanting to spoil the moment. "I'm fine."

"How about some coffee? Or something to eat?"

"You actually cook down there?" He'd pointed out the virtues of the stove, but she had assumed it was more for warming things up, fixing light meals.

"Like a master chef. Hold on, I'll get us a snack."

Before Laura could stop him and remind him about

supervising, he was gone. But not for long. He soon came up, juggling two steaming mugs of apple cider and a plate of donuts along with another sweater tossed over his forearm. He'd taken off his suit jacket and pulled on a heavy sweater over his shirt. He looked like a sailor except for the outline of his gun in its holster.

"Here, snuggle up." He tossed her the extra sweater.

"This is what you call cooking?" Laura teased after she'd pulled on the garment and reached for her food.

"Beggars shouldn't be choosers. It's a small stove."

"Actually it tastes delicious," she said, taking a bite of the donut and wrapping her fingers around the mug for warmth. She hadn't realized how cold she'd gotten in the short time they had been on the water.

"I accept all accolades." Kyle lit a lantern and sat beside her, sipping his drink. "Watch the crumbs," he warned, handing her a napkin.

"Mmm." Laura brushed the remnants of the donut from her mouth. "Thanks."

"You're welcome." He stared at her lips for the longest time. What was wrong with them? Frowning, Laura wiped her mouth again.

As though catching himself, Kyle turned away and nodded to other boats in the distance and to the harbor that had magically reappeared. "Look. Isn't it beautiful?"

Lights, like millions of stars, dotted the area. "Yes," Laura agreed.

"This is the time I like best, when the day disappears and the night begins. It's like a whole other world out here. All the big city problems seem so far away, almost nonexistent."

He was right. Laura even forgot her fear and relaxed, sitting silently, listening and looking. Off in the distance she could hear the traffic, but the horns were muffled, and the stench of the automobile exhaust was replaced by clean, slightly damp air. Here and there a fish splashed. Waves slapped against the hull, and the boat continued to bob gently up and down.

Kyle put one foot up on the bench and leaned back against the rail. He seemed so totally at ease, so in his element that Laura could almost believe he was part of this almost surrealistic world. By the light of the lantern his dark hair gleamed with ebony highlights.

"See what I mean?" he said after a while.

"Yes," she murmured. "Yes, I do."

He glanced at her. Then very softly he said, "You feel it, don't you, Laura? The magic?"

She wasn't quite certain about magic, but he was certainly weaving a spell. Perhaps he was the Water Witch. "Yes."

"There's something about the night and the stars and the wind," he went on softly, reaching to brush her hair back. The breeze whipped her long locks in her face but Laura couldn't move. She sat paralyzed by his voice and the night and his nearness. "Something so tenuous, fragile," he went on huskily. "Something not quite real."

At that moment he wasn't real. Nothing was real, she told herself, except the night and the moment. She shivered as he stroked his thumb back and forth across her cheek. His fingers were hot, like the sun, burning her skin.

"Laura?"

"Yes?"

He leaned toward her. She was certain he was going to kiss her, and she didn't know what to think or what to do. His face, shadowed by light, drew closer and closer...

"Laura, I—" His lips were but a breath away. She swallowed the lump of fear in her throat.

"Yes?" she said again, hoarsely.

All of a sudden, as though catching himself, he drew back. "God, I'm sorry, Laura. I didn't mean for that to happen."

Neither had Laura. Yet nothing had happened. Nothing really, except that she'd wanted his embrace, yearned for it. Startled by her reaction to him, she jumped up and went to the rail. She was still holding the mug in her hand and she didn't know what to do with it. She looked around.

"I'll make some more cider," he said, rising, too.

She glanced at the cup. "I—this is fine."

"You seem cold."

"I am." Cold and desperately hurt. There was a long, awkward silence. Laura looked out over the water. Finally Kyle moved behind her. She could sense his presence like fire in the night.

"I'm sorry, Laura," he said again.

For some silly reason the hurt cut deeper. Perhaps it was the darkness. The intensity of the days they'd shared, now and last fall. She turned back to him. "For what?"

"I had no right to touch you."

She shrugged. "Don't worry about it. People touch each other all the time."

"I had no right to kiss you."

"You didn't kiss me, Kyle," she corrected. "You turned away from me."

"I hurt you, didn't I?"

Should she tell the truth? She hurt so badly she couldn't describe it. "Yes."

"I'm sorry."

She laughed, and it was almost a bitter sound. "Why?"

"I don't want to hurt you, Laura."

"That's the way it goes, I guess." She laughed again. "The funny thing is, I'm not tainted. I don't even have a disease. It may be hard to believe, but Tony Calimara was very picky about his women."

"You think . . . ?" He seemed stunned by her revelation. "Laura, I didn't mean it that way!"

"No? How did you mean it, Kyle? How else could you mean it?" She sighed and stared off into the distance. "I think we should go back now. The sunset was super but it's getting late."

"Don't you think we should talk?"

"About what? Our quirks? I collect thimbles."

"You're angry."

She gave another sigh. "I'm tired. It's been a long day. Tomorrow's going to be even longer."

Kyle was still standing behind her, so close she could feel the heat of his body. "Let me into your life, Laura," he said softly. "Let me help you."

All of a sudden Laura saw red. Damn him! As the waves lapped harder the hurt stabbed deeper. She felt destroyed, and suddenly very, very angry. "Why?" she asked, whipping around to face him. "Why should I let you into my life? You're afraid to touch me." She held out her arm and gave a short, wild laugh. She was getting out of control but she couldn't help it. Too much had happened, too many people had hurt her. For too many days and weeks and months she'd pretended. "Look. Feel. You won't catch anything. I was raped.

Raped," she repeated quietly. "My body was violated, but I'm still a human being with wants and needs."

"Laura, I understand."

Did he? "Be honest, Kyle. Did you want to kiss me just now?"

"Laura, don't—"

"Please answer me," she said calmly, yet she felt anything but calm. "Did you want to kiss me just now?"

"Yes," he said at last.

"Did you want to touch me?"

"Yes."

"How? How did you want to touch me?"

"Laura, this is silly."

"Is it?" Laura wasn't certain what was happening to her, what was driving her, but once she had started she couldn't stop. All the anger and hurt and resentment she had bottled up over the months suddenly boiled over, and she lashed out at him. "Did you want to touch my breasts? Did you want to hold my body against yours?"

"Laura, I—"

"Why is it silly to want a man to kiss you?" she went on as if he hadn't spoken. "To touch you? Kiss me, Kyle."

"I can't."

"Why?" She moved closer to him, touching him. "Because I was raped? Kiss me, Kyle. Kiss me the way you would have kissed me if I hadn't been raped."

"Laura—"

"Do it," she commanded, reaching up and pulling his face down to hers. "Touch me, Kyle. Kiss me. Do something. Help me."

Maybe it was her cry for help, her hysterical need for reassurance, or maybe it was desire, Laura wasn't sure. But something broke Kyle's resistance, and with an agonized sigh deep in his throat, he pressed his mouth to hers almost brutally.

For all her pleas, her declarations of need, her protestations of hurt, the impact of his embrace was devastating to Laura's senses. As he groaned and gathered her to his body, emotions churned through her, conflicting emotions, battling, pulsing, pounding, tearing her apart. Fear, revulsion, need, pleasure, desire—they all warred for dominance, and she shuddered in reaction.

"Oh, Laura."

Kyle was the one to pull away. Holding her by the shoulders, he stood staring at her with a distraught expression while she panted for breath.

"Laura, I'm sorry."

Turning away, she ran a trembling hand through her hair. What had she expected? Instant desire? Passion? Love? How could she have made such a fool of herself? She laughed shakily, trying to make light of the situation. "Well, that was certainly honest."

"Laura—"

"Excuse me," she interrupted, trying to pull herself together. It wasn't his fault she had been raped. Why had she pushed him beyond his limits? Why had she let him kiss her? She glanced around. She had to get away. She had to get control of herself. "Is there a washroom on board this boat? I think I need to touch up my lipstick."

"Laura, listen to me."

She was growing frantic. "You wouldn't want me to put on my lipstick right here on deck, would you, Kyle?"

"Laura, please."

He started to take her hand but she snatched it away. "Don't."

"Laura—"

"Don't touch me!" She gasped when she realized what she'd said. "God, I'm sorry. I must sound like a schizophrenic. I'm tainted. I'm not tainted. Touch me. Don't touch me."

"I'm sorry."

"Dammit, Kyle," she said, dropping all pretense, "would you please stop apologizing and just tell me where the damned washroom is?"

"Below deck. Past my bunk and to the right."

"Thank you."

Just barely holding herself together, Laura placed her mug carefully on the seat, rushed down the steps leading into the cabin, and down the hall into the tiny bathroom. There weren't any lanterns lit and it was dark below deck, but she made her way through on pure mettle. Closing the door behind her, she leaned against the wall and let herself fall apart.

What a stupid thing to do. Kyle Patterson was her boss. He'd given her a chance, and she had just proved she wasn't ready. What if she overreacted during the assignment, like she had moments ago? She supposed what bothered her the most was the embarrassment. She'd thrown herself at him and then reacted like a silly teenager. But she'd been so frightened. And now she was so confused.

He confused her. He was an attractive man, the first man she'd been attracted to in months. And she'd blown it. Laura sat in the washroom for several minutes. She heard him come below deck and move around in the next room. She had to face him sometime. With a philosophical shrug, she opened the door.

He was standing near the stove. He'd lit a lantern and

brought down their mugs. He glanced at her. "I've heated some more apple cider."

How did one apologize for behaving like an idiot, she wondered. She untied her life preserver and handed it to him. "If you don't mind, I think I'll pass," she answered. "It was delicious, though. Do you think we could head back to shore now? It's really getting late."

If he heard her, he didn't respond to her question. He took the life jacket and tossed it into a corner. "I've put down the anchor."

What did that mean? It meant she was a captive audience, she realized moments later when he said, "Your fiancé broke off your engagement because you were raped, didn't he?"

There was no sense lying now, she realized. "Yes."

"What was his name?"

"Does it matter?"

"No. I'd just like to know his name so I can think of him as other than 'jerk' or 'he.'"

"Nick Wyndam."

"Did you love him?"

"I thought I loved him."

"Do you ever talk about it, Laura?"

She supposed she could pretend she didn't know what he was referring to, but that probably wouldn't dissuade him. "Yes, sometimes." To her therapist. To Cassie.

"Could we talk?"

But never to a man. It was early in their relationship for emotional issues, confrontations, but they'd just been quite emotional. Things had happened quickly between them, so she wasn't surprised at his question, just uncomfortable.

"I'm sorry, Kyle." She busied herself picking lint

from her blouse. "None of this was your fault, and I shouldn't have thrown myself at you like that. It's really out of character for me. I don't know what's the matter with me tonight. Maybe it's the boat." She forced herself to smile. "The magic," she added lamely. When he didn't answer she said, "I hope you'll still give me a chance at the operation."

"The operation has nothing to do with what happened up there on deck, Laura. That was between us. You and me."

Man and woman, she thought. She glanced at him and said honestly, "It proved that I'm not reliable."

"Because you overreacted?"

"Yes."

"I overreacted, too. Sometimes people do that. I'm still willing to be your partner."

"Thank you." She was surprised, and she was truly grateful.

"But we still have to talk," he went on.

"Kyle—"

"This is difficult for me, Laura. It's difficult for me to explain, but I feel things for you, things that I'm afraid would frighten you." He paused, as though uncertain about how much to tell her. "This may sound hokey, but to put it politely, when it comes to you, my thoughts are impure."

She smiled at him. He certainly had a unique way of phrasing things. She didn't deserve his understanding, the chance he was giving her. "I—"

"No, let me finish." He shoved his hands in his pockets and started to pace back and forth across the small area. "We need to get things straight between us, Laura."

"For the operation?"

He nodded. "Yes, and for us personally. We've only known each other a short time, but we'd be fools if we didn't admit that there's more than an operation between us. If we're going to have a chance, any chance at all, as partners or as more than partners, we've got to get things out in the open. I have to know how you feel and you have to know how I feel. We have to stop lying to each other and pussyfooting around. We have to be honest. We have to talk."

"All right," she answered quietly. "What do you want to talk about?"

"First of all I feel responsible for you," he admitted, "for what happened to you that night last fall."

"It wasn't your fault," she assured him. "It just happened."

"It wasn't your fault, either. But it was my detail you were working. It was my plan, and it went wrong."

"You don't have to feel guilty, Kyle."

"Don't you understand, Laura? I can't help how I feel. I'm all mixed up inside, maybe as mixed up as you are. I feel things for you, things I'm not sure you're ready for. But I feel them. I've felt them all along, while you were engaged to that Wyndam jerk and now, too, and I think you feel them, also. And you're just as frightened as I am." He leaned against the stove and looked directly at her. "Lots of feeling there," he joked.

"Look, I'm going to be honest," he went on. "Brutally honest. The truth is, Laura, despite being your partner and despite what happened to you, I want to make love to you. I want to kiss you until you beg for mercy. I want to know you, completely, totally. I want to feel your body quivering, beneath mine, but I know you've been hurt. I know you've been raped. I listened, while he violated you, and I couldn't help you."

"I've gone past that, Kyle. I've gotten over that part of it."

"I haven't. And it's killing me inside." He paused, sighing heavily. "The reason I don't want to touch you is that I couldn't stand it if you cringed from me. When I felt you shudder earlier, I wanted to kill him. I wanted to destroy Tony Calimara with my bare hands."

"And it went against everything you believe in."

"Yes."

"Very uncoplike. I know the feeling. It goes away."

"Does it? Isn't that what you're afraid of, Laura? Of blowing it when you're faced with a situation that reminds you of that night?"

Laura was amazed at how astute he was. "Yes."

"We're quite a pair, aren't we?"

She laughed. "Yes, we are."

"We'll manage," he said. "I'd be willing to bet that we'll even arrest ourselves a few criminals."

What about their personal relationship? How were they going to handle that? "I like to roller-skate," Laura said after a long silence.

He frowned. "What?"

"My hobbies," she explained. "I like to roller-skate."

He gave a short laugh and shook his head as though in disbelief. "You know something, Laura Davis? You're quite a woman and you're quite a cop."

"And this is going to be one hell of an operation," she finished for him.

He looked deeply into her eyes, and an electric feeling surged between them like live wires sparking with fire. "I hope so. I sure as hell hope so."

CHAPTER FIVE

KYLE DIDN'T SAY MUCH on the way back to the docks, and neither did Laura. The highly charged emotions they had just experienced seemed to quiet them both. While he steered the boat, she sat on the padded bench and watched the harbor lights change from bright stars to ugly, glaring light bulbs, the magic turning to harsh reality. After securing the *Water Witch* against the pier, Kyle helped her from the craft and side by side, they walked to his car. Since it had turned cool, Laura was still wearing his sweater.

"I'd take a bus home," she said as he assisted her into the vehicle, "but I don't think there are any that go to my apartment from here."

"Don't worry about it. It's no problem to take you home."

"You have to come back."

"I knew that when I invited you to see the sunset."

Laura didn't remark, and the small exchange seemed to be the sum total of their conversation for the rest of the ride to her apartment. Yet she didn't feel awkward. In fact, she felt quite comfortable with Kyle Patterson at her side.

Too comfortable, perhaps?

Not wanting to consider that possibility (after all, what could she do if it was true?), Laura leaned back against the seat and watched the Chicago neighborhoods. The city was so diverse, a melting pot of young and old, rich and poor, modern and ancient, from the Water Tower to the Sears Tower, from the lakefront condos to the tenements, from the neighborhoods to the Loop. Here and there small ethnic groups had taken root, and as they drove, the signs advertising products changed from Spanish to Polish to Chinese to Italian to Yugoslavian and to English again.

They crossed the bridge by the WGN studios, and Kyle turned down her street. "Don't forget that we're going to be qualifying at the range in the morning," he reminded her as he maneuvered into a parking space in front of her building.

"Should I wear my uniform?"

"No, we're going to be on the street in the afternoon. You won't need to qualify from your holster. I thought we'd do some freestyle shooting."

She started to get out of the car, but he came around and opened her door. "I'll walk you to your door."

"I can manage."

"I know you can." He smiled. "Let me be polite."

Politeness was the least of Laura's concerns. In spite of their earlier discussion, she wasn't certain how they stood with each other personally. Would he try to *kiss* her good night? And if he did, how would she react? On the boat, when he'd kissed her, she'd panicked. But they had talked for hours afterward. Had they talked out her fears? What about his fears?

Kyle didn't seem at all anxious. He casually placed his hand on her back, guiding her along as they headed up her front steps. Perhaps he had the right idea. The best way to approach the situation was directly. When they got to the entrance she turned to him and smiled.

"Thanks again, Kyle. The sunset was lovely."

"You're welcome," he answered. He had shoved his hands in his pockets, and he nodded toward the vestibule. "Sure you'll get in all right?"

"I'll be fine."

"Well, I guess I'll say good-night, then."

"Yes, good-night."

Although she said the words, Laura didn't make a move to leave. The streetlight played on his features much as the moonlight had on the boat, and she found herself staring at the planes and hollows of his face.

"Laura?"

She stared at his lips as they descended to hers. "Yes?"

"I'm going to kiss you."

She was unable to move. "I know."

"I won't hurt you."

Despite the fact that he had warned her and despite the fact that she welcomed his embrace and even yearned for it, Laura felt the same momentary panic as she had earlier. "Kyle—"

"Trust me, Laura," he murmured as their breath mingled together. "Let me kiss you."

She stood stock-still.

"Let me kiss you," he repeated huskily. "Let me show you how it can feel."

With his head tilted slightly, he leaned closer.

And closer.

Laura's heart pounded hard in her chest. She moistened her lips automatically, and at last his mouth met hers. Barely. He brushed his lips across hers so lightly he might have used a feather, yet the contact was electric. Her pulse skyrocketed. He paused, turning his head the other way and teasing her again with his lips, with tiny nips at her mouth. She wanted nothing more than to pull his head down until his lips crushed hers. She wanted to be kissed until she couldn't think or hear or feel or need any more. Until she begged for mercy.

"Laura," he said hoarsely as she tilted her head back and moaned, making a tiny noise of pleasure deep in her throat.

Taking the invitation she offered, Kyle trailed his lips along her neck, kissing her lightly there, too, yet barely touching her. His hand, so warm and strong, cupped her head and caressed her cheek. He moved his fingers down along her throat to the top of her breast. She didn't move. She didn't flinch. She felt as though she'd been caught up in a storm from which she did not want to escape. Pleasure coursed through her like a red-hot tempest.

Kyle drew away. "I'd better go," he said, his tone ragged and husky. "Before I can't."

Laura drew a shaky breath and answered, "Yes. That's a good idea."

He touched her cheek lightly and brushed back a stray lock of hair. "Good-night, Laura."

"Good-night," she whispered, turning to go inside. Then she noticed that Kevin was looking at them through a window. She'd forgotten the children's bedroom was in the front. Had the child seen and heard everything? Laura wondered. But he seemed more concerned with getting her attention.

"Psst," he called. "Occifer Lady-Fwiendly. Is that you, Occifer Lady-Fwiendly?"

"Yes, it's me, Kevin," Laura whispered back. "What are you doing up? Why aren't you asleep?"

"I been waiting for you."

"You shouldn't be talking out the window. It's dangerous."

"It's all right," he answered. "It's to you."

How could she respond to that?

"We're still punished," he went on whispering, pressing closer to the screen. Laura could see his blue eyes now and his printed pajamas. "My mom would get mad if she knew I was still up. Whata ya been doing?"

This time she wasn't about to answer. "Nothing. What did you want?"

"Are you ever gonna look in your refrigerator?"

"Attila," Kyle murmured from behind her.

Laura tried to stifle a grin. "I did look, Kevin."

His eyes grew big and round and he put his hand over his mouth. "Did you see the monster?"

"Yes," she answered gravely, playing along. "I certainly did."

"Were you scared?"

She put her hand over her heart and pretended to gasp. "Terribly."

The child giggled, but then he said very seriously, "It's not mine. It's Shawnie's. I gotta give the monster back to him."

"How about if I bring it down to you in the morning?" Laura suggested.

"He wants it back before the morning."

"You can't give it to him now," Laura pointed out.

Kevin thought about that for a moment. "I wasn't s'posed to have it. My mommy doesn't like me playing with it. She don't like slime."

"Oh," Laura said. "Well what do you want me to do with it?"

"If you put it in the milk box tonight I can get it out in the morning before my mommy sees it. I gotta go to nursery school. I can give it to Shawnie there."

"Okay," Laura said, willing to be part of the conspiracy only because he was so sincere. "I'll put it in the milk box right now."

"How?" he asked.

Laura blinked in confusion. "What do you mean, how?"

"You can't touch it," he said. "You're s'posed to be scared of it. It's a monster."

"Oh." Laura frowned. "Right."

"Tell you what, Kevin," Kyle broke in. "How about if I go up and get Attila and put it in the milk box for you?"

Kevin beamed. "Could you?"

"Sure. Don't worry about a thing. I'll take care of it. You go to bed, now. And don't talk to anybody out the window any more."

The boy nodded. "I won't."

Laura stared at Kyle after Kevin closed the window and pulled down his shade. "What a way to get into my apartment," she joked.

He frowned. "What do you mean?"

"If I didn't know better I'd swear that was as smooth a line as they come."

He seemed genuinely hurt by her accusation. "I'm surprised you'd think that, Laura," he said softly. "I've been honest with you, and I would never hand you a line. It wouldn't be fair to either of us."

Struck by the sincerity of his expression, she knew he was speaking the truth. Of all the things she had to fear from him—and there was plenty to fear—a line wasn't one of them. She also knew that when he came to her bed, it would be by invitation. And he knew it, too. She could tell by the way he was looking at her. This surely was going to be one hell of an operation.

"You're very good with kids," she said.

"So are you."

"A quirk?"

"I doubt it."

"I want several."

"So do I."

Although they were talking about children, this discussion wasn't really about children at all. It was about the two of them, their needs and compatability.

"Good," Laura said. "Come on up." She unlocked the door and stepped inside. There was a note stuck in her mailbox—more than likely a message from Cassie. She took it and started up the steps. "Attila's in the fridge. Wait a minute. I'll get him."

"Do you want me to do the honors? He is a monster."

She smiled. "Okay, you can go ahead. Then I won't have to touch him." She led the way into her apartment and showed him the refrigerator.

"Laura, he's wonderful," Kyle said. "Look at him."

Laura had tossed the note on a table and followed Kyle to the kitchen. She stood leaning against the doorframe as he took the monster from the refrigerator. It looked just as fierce as ever. Slimy green goo still dripped from its jowls.

"Ugh," she said.

With his other hand Kyle reached to wipe the slime from the shelves, letting it sift between his fingers. "Look at this stuff. It's great."

"Yuk."

"Girls never could appreciate good toys." He glanced at her. "Want to try it?"

"No," she said, going for a paper towel. "I think it's disgusting." The goo started running down his hand and dripping to the floor. "And I won't even comment about your sexist remark."

Kyle laughed. "Better hurry with those paper towels."

Laura tried to put the paper towels under his hand but he tilted the monster and the goo dripped faster. "Ugh," she said again. "This is gross. How can you touch it? Here, let me help."

The slime had gotten onto the sleeves of his shirt. She started to dab at the green liquid, but all of a sudden she looked up at him. When had her touch become a caress? For she was caressing him. The thick, dark hairs prickled her fingers sensuously and heat spread through her as she moved her hand slowly up his forearm, over the sinewy muscles she'd watched in the briefing room. Would he notice?

"I don't think I'm doing much good."

"You're doing fine." Kyle felt it, too, she realized, and the moment stretched forever as he stared down into her eyes. He caressed her cheek. Neither of them noticed the green goo that was smeared on his hand until a small portion of it dripped on her collarbone.

Although she glanced at it, she didn't move. Still with her hand on his arm, she watched him, mesmerized by the intensity of his gaze as he watched the green goo run gradually down her chest and disappear into the V of her blouse. When he looked back up at her face, he didn't have to speak the words for her to know that he wanted to trail his finger along the same path, and then his lips.

"I wouldn't dare," was all he said.

With a sense of surprise, Laura realized that she might not have stopped him. "Why not?"

"Things have gotten out of hand, Laura," he said in a low, quiet tone. "This is a no-win situation. I'm damned if I do and I'm damned if I don't. I think I'd better leave."

Laura wasn't ordinarily given to impulse, but suddenly she smiled and slowly traced the path of green with her own finger. "Before you go," she said softly. Then, still holding him with her gaze, she trailed the finger across his hand and over his arm.

"You're *teasing* him," she could almost hear Dr. Lowenstein say. "This is progress, Laura."

Although he held his breath in slightly, Kyle didn't blink an eye. He grabbed her wrist, though, stopping her. "What was that all about?"

The goo left on his hand felt sensuous where it slid over hers. "Honesty."

"You wanted to touch me?"

"Yes."

"You want me to touch you?"

She shrugged. Her heart was pounding so hard that her blood had started to roar in her ears. "Maybe. Not yet."

"Naked."

"What?"

"One of my quirks," he explained. "I sleep naked."

"Do you think I need to know that in order to be your partner?"

"No. But I didn't need to know that you like to roller-skate in order to be your partner, either."

"No, you didn't."

"And we sure as hell didn't need to complicate matters with this mutual attraction."

"No, we didn't."

"But it's happening." Still holding the monster but not caring where the slime went, he placed his hands on the wall behind her at either side of her head. "This may be a tactical error on my part, Officer Davis, but I'm going to kiss you," he murmured. "Hard." Although his body didn't touch hers, or perhaps because of it, she became even more aware of his hard leanness. "And then I'm going to get the hell out of here."

Laura slept fitfully, feeling too warm for such a cool spring night. Her body was flushed and she kept tossing and turning, resenting the nightgown that twisted around her legs and restricted her movements. She wanted to rip it off and lay naked on the cool sheets.

She punched the pillow, instead. It had been a long time since she'd been attracted to a man, let alone had the attraction disturb her and interfere with her sleep. Yet this was what she was feeling. And it was building.

Following through on his pledge, Kyle had kissed her and then left, monster in hand. Not that she'd wanted him to stay—not yet anyway. She wasn't ready for a relationship, sexual or otherwise, and both of them knew it. But his mouth had aroused feelings in her that she didn't know still existed. The kiss was as real to her now as it had been an hour ago. She touched her lips. They still tingled, and she could almost feel his mouth on hers, his tongue darting inside, demanding.

She had to admire his honesty. He'd kissed her very

hard, and when he'd leaned his body against hers, trapping her, she had felt his erection against her leg. There was no question that he wanted her. The moment was intense. Only the fact that she'd been so aroused had kept her from shuddering with fear.

She punched the pillow again. Now that same arousal was keeping her awake.

The ringing telephone woke Laura. Who could be calling at this hour? The alarm clock read five A.M. She must have finally fallen asleep. Groggily she reached for the bedside phone. "Hello."

"Good morning." Cassie's voice floated through the wires. "Didn't you get my note?"

Laura yawned. "Yes, I got it, but I didn't read it. What are you doing up?"

"Getting ready for work. It takes me longer than you. I have to apply most of my beauty. You know, Laura, people generally leave notes for a reason. Weren't you even curious?"

"I'm sorry. Did you want something?"

"Just to tell you that I'm going to be busy tonight. I've got a hot date."

Laura sat up in the bed and crossed her legs under her. "Who with?"

"A construction worker. Actually, he owns the firm, but he was running around in a hard hat and tight jeans yesterday. I had to arrest him for not having a building permit. The guy's built like a brick outhouse. I can hardly wait to see his phallic symbol."

A smile twitched at Laura's lips. Her friend was so outspoken. One of these days Cassie was going to get in trouble. "It's phallus," she corrected. "It's not a symbol when it's on a person."

"Whatever. Where were you?"

"Last night? With Kyle on his boat."

There was a long pause. "You aren't rushing things, are you, Laura?"

She wasn't, but "things" were happening rather fast. "No."

"Just be careful."

"Doesn't that remind you of something like the pot and the kettle?" Laura asked.

"Now *you've* got the analogy wrong, but I'll be careful, too," Cassie said. "Hey, I've got to go. I'll see you later."

"Have fun."

"You, too."

Since she was already awake, Laura decided to shower and get ready for work. She'd taken one shower last night to get the green slime off of her body, but she could use another one today in order to stay alert. They were going to be shooting, and she would have to be razor sharp. Although Kyle believed in her ability, she wanted to give everyone else on the detail reason to believe in her, too. She wanted to show them that she was capable, including being able to shoot her weapon better than all the rest of them.

Because they were going to be downtown again, at the central police station, Laura dressed casually, in a skirt and blouse. Like the day before, everyone had already arrived when she walked into the station. The target range was in the basement. The area was soundproofed with tiles and padding, and it was darkened, except for the targets, which were lit and which moved and changed at the flick of a switch in the control room.

Police officers used the range every day, qualifying

for the street and testing their ability. Kyle stood near a khaki-clad officer who was obviously from the SWAT team and held an Uzi submachine gun in front of him.

All business, Kyle barely glanced at her as someone handed her earphones to muffle the noise. "Glad you're here, Laura." He nodded to the officer. "We're ready to begin."

Without fanfare the man whirled to the target, squeezing the trigger. Laura was already wearing the earphones but she could still hear the rapid staccato sound of the gunfire. Before she could take a breath, the officer had emptied the clip and shoved in another. In a fraction of a second, he emptied the second clip.

"This probably wasn't necessary," Kyle said when the man was done and the target had been destroyed, literally blown away. "You're all very aware of the fire-power of this weapon. I just wanted to remind you that it's in the hands of people who intend to misuse it and that we need to catch them before anyone gets hurt. Now, we'll all take turns." He glanced at Laura. "Mind being first?"

Perhaps he was also trying to assure the others that she was capable of performing on this operation. She stepped forward without hesitation. "Sure."

Laura carried a .38 revolver, Chicago Police Department issue. It was a small weapon, easily concealed, easy to handle, and yet with enough firepower to stop a speeding car or a fleeing felon. She'd been taught the FBI method of shooting, and she turned to the target, ensconced in a long, tunnellike structure. "Now!"

The target lit up, moved forward, then back just as quickly, simulating someone running away. She had only a moment to aim. She fired. More targets popped up and she kept firing.

When the lights indicating the end of her turn went on, Kyle examined the cardboard silhouettes. Each one had a hole through the bull's-eye. "Very good."

"Thank you."

He turned to Stan. "Ready?"

The MEG officer glanced at Laura with new respect. "She's going to be hard to beat."

No one did beat her. Kyle came close, missing the center of a bull's-eye by only a hair. He holstered his gun and turned to them after he had examined his own cardboard figure. "Looks like we're ready. Any questions?"

Jim shook his head. "Let's hit the streets."

"Fine." Kyle nodded and handed out their driver's licenses and passports. "We'll meet at the Federal Building later tonight to exchange information and see what we've come up with." From his pants' pocket, Kyle pulled out several maps and handed one to each person. The west side of the city had been divided into small two- or three-block areas. "Laura and I will take the north sector. Sam and Phyllis, take the south. Jim and Stan hit the east. We'll worry about the last sector in the morning." He held out his arm as though waiting for her to join him. "Laura."

She walked to his side. When everyone had left she placed her hand on his arm. "Kyle, I wanted to thank you for being so detached earlier."

He frowned at her. "What do you mean?"

She shrugged. "For treating me as if we're just cops. For acting as if nothing has happened between us." Even to Laura, her statement sounded conflicting. Nothing had happened between them, but in a way everything had happened between them. "I appreciate it."

"We are just cops, Laura," he answered, "at any time that we're working the operation. Hungry? I thought we'd stop for lunch."

Sometimes he confused her. "What about the street? Don't we have to talk to people about the guns?"

"The people will still be there when we're done." He smiled. "Come on. Even cops are allowed to eat. And we never did get around to that newspaper last night," he went on, steering her out of the building. "I thought you were going to give me some advice about an apartment."

"What advice?"

He shrugged. "Like get out of the Wilson Arms?"

"Get out of the Wilson Arms."

He laughed. "I guess I deserved that one."

"You did."

"You know something, Laura?" He looked at her with new respect. "I was really impressed by how darned fast you are on the draw."

But not fast enough, she thought, or she would never have let him into her life. She would never have let him come near her, kiss her, and touch her. She would never have confronted him last night. Being with Kyle Patterson was like pouring gasoline near a spark and waiting for the explosion. They were barreling nonstop into a tempest and there wasn't a damn thing she could do to prevent it. She knew it as surely as she was standing here breathing. The worst part of it was, she wasn't certain she *wanted* to prevent it.

CHAPTER SIX

LUNCH WAS A HURRIED AFFAIR in a crowded restaurant near the police station. When they had finished eating and started their coffee, Kyle placed a newspaper on the table and opened it to the classified section. "By the way," he said, "I meant what I said about you being quick on the draw. You've got a very good aim."

"Thank you."

"Do you target practice much?"

Lately she had, she'd wanted so desperately to get back on MEG. But she'd also come down to the range just to shoot, just to get out her aggressions and diffuse her anger. She'd held in a lot of anger the last few months. "Yes, I do."

"You should work with weapons. Ever consider joining the Bureau?"

She shook her head. "I like being a cop."

"Undercover."

"Yes. Working the beat was awful."

"Somebody's gotta do it."

"I'm glad it's not me." The waitress hadn't cleared their dishes yet, and absently Laura picked up a french fry from her plate and munched it. "My friend Cassie doesn't mind. She likes the street."

"She sounds like an interesting character."

Laura smiled. "She is. You'll have to meet her one day."

"I'd like that."

At his low tone, she glanced up. When had they ceased being cops and become man and woman? All of a sudden she was very aware of him and of his eyes on her. She lowered the french fry and licked her lips nervously. "Why do you keep staring at me whenever I eat?"

"Are you sure you want to know?"

"We're supposed to be honest with each other."

"All right," he answered huskily. "I stare at you when you're eating because your mouth is magnificent. You do things with it that drive me wild."

Laura flushed. "Oh."

"I'm sorry," Kyle apologized. "I didn't mean to embarrass you."

She shrugged. "You didn't. Not really. I'm just not certain that's a compliment. It sounds so . . . sexual."

"Oh, it's a compliment, all right," he said. "And my thoughts *are* sexual. Honesty, you said," he added as though he was worried about her reaction.

"I see."

"Do you?" He was even more intense than ever as he nailed her with his gaze. "Then maybe you can tell me, Laura, what the hell are we going to do about this tension between us?"

When had their relationship escalated to this point? She didn't bother to deny his statement or to play coy. She couldn't. There was tension between them, and there was no sense in pretending it didn't exist. "I don't know."

"You're not ready." It was a statement of fact rather than a question, and he was right. She wasn't ready for an encounter.

"I'm sorry."

"Don't be. It'll happen eventually." He searched her face with his gaze. "You know that, don't you?"

As egotistical as his remark sounded, Laura knew he wasn't bragging. He'd merely spoken the truth, the truth that she'd already acknowledged and known all along, since that moment they had looked at each other seven months ago. Before the rape. What was going to happen between them was inevitable. It was just a matter of when. "Yes, I know."

His tone grew husky again. "Did you get the slime out of your blouse?"

"No," she answered. "I had to throw my blouse out."

"I had a hell of a time getting the stuff off my body."

"So did I." As she continued to stare at him, mesmerized by his gaze, Laura couldn't help imagining the two of them in the shower together.

He would be tanned, every inch of his body hard. The water would stream over him and the soap would feel sensuous in her hands while she slid it over his shoulders, along his chest, across his abdomen, then down . . . to his hardness. She would touch him, caress him. And he would caress her also and kiss her. The image was so vivid she felt herself grow warm.

Kyle must have had similar thoughts because he drew a ragged breath and shifted uncomfortably, ab-

ruptly glancing down into his coffee. "So," he said,
clearing his throat, "did Kevin find his monster this
morning?"

Laura knew he didn't care at that particular moment
whether the child had found the monster or not, she
didn't care, either. But she answered anyway, realizing
that they both needed to readjust their thoughts. "Gra-
cious," Dr. Lowenstein would say, "now you're having
lurid thoughts? In a restaurant, no less? Laura! How
shocking!" But actually the doctor wouldn't be shocked,
she'd be delighted. "You'll get past these barriers yet,
Laura," would be her words.

Laura cleared her throat, too. "When I left this morning the monster was gone."

"Good."

"There was slime all over the milk box, though," she
went on. She needed to get up and move, to get herself
together. "The child is not good at covering his crimes.
I have a feeling he's going to get caught despite our
efforts."

"A criminal in the making?"

"More like a child in deep trouble with his mother."
Laura gestured to the paper. "You'll never find an apartment if we keep putting off looking at those ads."

"There's not much here. Just a couple of columns."
He handed her a page.

She quickly scanned the "For Rent" section. "There
are a few that sound promising." When he responded
with a chuckle, she looked up at him and saw that he
was reading the section he had in his hand. "What are
you laughing at?"

"Personals column."

"No wonder."

"Here's a kinky one. Charming middle-aged woman

looking for young stud with lots of stamina." Knowing deep down inside that she should keep her mouth shut, and yet feeling terribly mischievous, she smiled at him. "Think you qualify?"

He gave her a long, searching look that confirmed that she should have followed her first instincts. "I don't know. You think I do?"

There it was again, that tension between them, the shift to mutual awareness. Laura wiggled nervously in her seat.

"How would I know?" Hoping to diffuse the situation, she glanced back at the paper, studying it as though it were a document from the Supreme Court. "Here's one, but the address is near the Wilson Arms."

Kyle also let the moment slip past. He took up the page and said, "We could go look at this one tomorrow. One bedroom flat, completely furnished, kitchen, dinette, skylight. All utilities. Dynamic view of the lake. It seems to have everything."

"Where?"

"It says Gold Coast area."

"Good address," Laura remarked. "Got lots of money?"

"Hmm. Well. I guess it's back to the lady looking for the stud. Let's see, she's offering breakfast."

Laura laughed. "What? Oats?"

He laughed, too. Then he sobered and said, "You don't laugh much, do you, Laura?"

She'd never thought much about it. She shrugged. "I guess not."

"I'd like to change that."

Laura knew that he was serious. So was she, for the moment. Then smiling devilishly, she picked up a french fry and rubbed it slowly back and forth across her lower lip. She surprised herself at how bold she was getting. "Unfortunately, you've made it clear that's not all you want to change, Agent Patterson."

A grin twitched at his mouth. "I keep telling you I'm just a regular nice guy doing good deeds all day long."

"You've told me no such thing."

"I'm telling you now."

She popped the french fry in her mouth. "And I'm Mary Poppins."

"You," he said, sighing and rising to leave, "are incredibly sexy." He flipped some change on the table. "As well as cruel. Come on, let's get to work before I lose control and call your bluff."

Laura didn't feel in the least bit threatened. It was strange, but all she felt was pleasure. It delighted her to realize that she had healed to the point that after seven months of avoiding all thoughts of sex, at last she was comfortable enough with a man to tease him, and to actually relish the moments. And she was even more delighted to know that she turned him on.

But back on the street Kyle was all business. Although they were posing as man and wife, he didn't allow the expression of any sexual nuance. The way he acted she could have been sexless.

They talked with person after person, walked to shop after shop, pretending, asking about weapons. No one seemed to be interested. Each person they approached shook their heads.

"I don't know nothin' about bullets, mister," a pawn-shop owner remarked when Kyle asked about getting some ammunition. "Never heard of the stuff."

Kyle handed the man a piece of paper with the office phone number scrawled on it. "You can reach us here if you ever do hear of some weapons." He took out a wad of money. "We're willing to pay a premium price."

The man stared at the money. "You buying something?"

"My wife likes that ring." Kyle pointed to a cheap pearl that wasn't worth ten dollars. "Don't you, honey?"

Laura nodded. "Yes. It's lovely."

"She's got good taste." The man pulled the ring from the case and handed it to her. "So what do you need bullets for?"

"A revolution."

"Got something against the Canadian government?"

"I'm tired of paying taxes."

"You should move to the United States, mister. We get robbed blind here. Why do you think I'd know anything about ammunition?"

"We've been hearing about you on the street."

The man turned ugly. "Who's talking?"

Kyle didn't back down. "Have we been hearing wrong?"

The man just glared at them. "How do I know you're not a cop?"

Kyle shrugged, peeling five hundred-dollar bills and placing them on the counter with his driver's license, which listed him as a Canadian citizen. "You don't. You have to take my word for it."

The man didn't bite, though. The money sat on the counter. Although he did pocket the phone number. "Did you want to buy something else?"

"I thought you said the ring was five hundred."

"You heard wrong, buddy. Three hundred's plenty. Now, if you don't want anything else, maybe you better get the hell out of here before people start talking. I can't afford to be busted for dealing with revolutionaries."

"Sure thing," Kyle said, placing his hand on Laura's back and escorting her to the door. "Keep in touch."

"Yeah. I'll give you a call."

It was too good to be true. When they got outside Laura glanced at Kyle. "What do you think?"

He shrugged. "I don't know. We'll find out in a few days. He seemed interested. He didn't take the extra money, but in a way that's a good sign. I think he might have some contacts and figure he'll get a lot more in the end."

"Could we be that lucky?"

"It does seem like a fluke."

"Something about him bothered me. Did you catch his name? It was on one of the cards he had lying on the counter."

"Morgan."

"That's what I thought."

"It's a common name," Kyle pointed out as he switched places with her, walking on the outside of the street. "Maybe you saw it somewhere."

"Could be." Laura smiled, remembering what he'd said about carrying his gun on the left. "I gather you were serious the other day about your quirks."

He smiled, too. "This one at least." Then he was all business again as he glanced at his watch and nodded to another pawnshop down the block. "We've got a few more minutes. Let's head for that shop over there."

They repeated the same act for several more pawn-brokers and several more contacts. At last Kyle headed for the car. "We better knock off for the day and meet the others. It'll take us a year to get back downtown." He glanced at her. "Tired?"

Laura nodded. "Yes, I am. I didn't sleep well last

night." She flushed. She had blurted the words out before she realized what she was admitting.

Kyle smiled. "Neither did I. I had a problem with dreams." He helped her into the car and got in his side. "I do sleep nude."

What did he want her to say? "I don't."

"Inhibitions?"

She shook her head. "I think I mentioned once I grew up in a house with six brothers."

"That's right, you did." He put the car in gear and pulled into the lane of traffic. "Do you ever miss home?"

"Sometimes. I visit a lot, whenever I can get away."

"What's it like?"

She shrugged. "It's nice. Small in comparison to Chicago."

"Does your family know what happened to you?"

One of the problems with Kyle Patterson was that he tossed off those zingers without batting an eyelash. Laura hesitated, though she wasn't certain why. "No."

"Why not?"

Why did he have to probe? "I don't know. I'm not sure. Both Cassie and Dr. Lowenstein insist that I'm repressing what happened. They tell me I need to talk about it, bring it out in the open."

"But?"

Again Laura wondered why it was that she could talk so freely to this man who only hours before had looked at her with lust in his eyes and spoken to her with seduction in his voice. Perhaps it was because he had been so open and honest with her, telling her he wanted her. Or perhaps it was because he did probe. "Bringing it out in the open isn't as easy as it sounds," she answered. "As far as my family is concerned, knowing about what happened to me would only worry them. They'd want me to come home."

"And you don't want to do that."

"I like Chicago. I do miss Kansas City sometimes, but I'm not a country girl."

"You're old-fashioned."

Where had he come up with that? "No, I'm not," she scoffed.

"Sure you are." Taking his gaze off the road for a moment he glanced at her. "You're straitlaced, straight-forward, and trusting."

"You make them seem like bad qualities."

"On the contrary, I think they're excellent qualities. I'm just surprised that with everything that's happened to you, you're still so . . . innocent."

She smiled. "I thought I was sexy."

"You are," he said. He glanced at her again. "And innocent."

"That's a contradiction."

"Why?" He glanced back to the road. "Can't a person be both at the same time?"

She wrinkled her forehead in thought. "I suppose."

"Believe me, Laura, it's exactly that quality in women that drives men wild."

"Really?" She leaned her head back and watched him steer the car. What was there about him that drove her wild with longing? She knew he'd had his share of lovers; women probably fell at his feet. Was it his overwhelming masculinity or the way he wore his dark hair longish at the neck? The body that resembled a Greek god? The sensuous eyes?

"Really," he reiterated.

Laura kept watching him. His hands clasped the wheel expertly and the muscles in his thighs flexed and tightened as he braked and accelerated while maneuvering through traffic. He had loosened his tie and unbuttoned the top of his shirt. Tiny dark hairs peeked from the opening—he would have a hairy chest. It was broad, like his shoulders, and lean. She'd felt it last night, when he'd pressed against her.

"Maybe," she agreed. "I guess I'm skeptical because no one has ever thought I was sexy before."

"What? You're kidding." He laughed, actually tossed back his head and laughed out loud.

She stared at him. "What's so funny?"

He shook his head. "Nothing."

But he was still amused. He was smiling.

"You laughed. What did I say that was so funny?"

"Laura, you just prove over and over again that you're old-fashioned and damned innocent. Any man who has ever looked at you would have to acknowledge that you're sexy."

Oddly the knowledge that men would find her sensuous pleased Laura. "No one's ever told me before."

"How about jerky Nick?"

She was surprised by the vehemence in his tone. "Why don't you like Nick?"

"He's a jerk. He jilted you."

"I might point out that you couldn't have kissed me last night if jerky Nick hadn't jilted me."

Kyle arched an eyebrow. "Don't count on it, Laura," he said in a low voice. "I think I would have kissed you, anyhow. Unfortunately I don't think I could have kept away from you, no matter who you were engaged to." He paused. "Or who you were married to."

"That bothers you, doesn't it?" She learned more and more about him with each passing moment. He was like a puzzle she was piecing together.

"Yes."

"Why?"

"Another man's woman should be off limits."

"I see." She paused. "Tell me about Detroit."

He gave her a brief glance but quickly returned his attention to traffic. "Why Detroit?"

"I'm interested. You grew up there, didn't you?"

"Yes, but I don't remember much about it except for the tenement housing. I was actually grateful for the Army."

"Was that your first time away from home?"

"The first time was when my sister and I were taken away from our parents when I was about ten, but we ended up in a worse section of the city."

She was sure that had to have affected him and the way he dealt with life. "What happened to your parents?"

"They died. Car accident."

"After you were taken away?"

"Yes."

"And your sister?"

"She fell in love and moved. I think I told you she lives in California now."

"Yes, I remember." Laura wasn't certain whether to probe further or whether he was uncomfortable talking about his family. Yet he hadn't held back with her. "Have you ever been in love, Kyle?"

They had reached the street where the Federal Building was located. He pulled into a nearby parking garage, found a space, shut off the engine, and turned to her. "No, I've never been in love."

"You've had relationships, though."

He nodded. "Yes."

"Lots?"

"Does it matter?"

She wasn't certain why it did matter or even how she would react to his answer. "I don't know."

"I think you're scared, Laura. I think you're looking for reasons to run away from what's happening between us."

Unfortunately his words had the ring of truth to them. "What is happening between us, Kyle?" she asked. "I'm not even sure of what's going on. We've known each other for only three days."

"So?"

She didn't know herself what she was trying to say. More than ever she was sorry she had confronted him last night, because then he'd kissed her and she'd wanted him. Things were moving so fast between them. All she'd thought of all day was how much she desired him. "So maybe we're imagining this."

"This? This what?"

"This . . ."

"Say it, Laura. This what?"

It was strange to her that they were sitting in a car in a dark garage talking so frankly. She found it terribly hard to speak the words. "This . . . sensuality," she said at last. "Wanting each other."

"Are you admitting that you want me?"

"I'm . . ." Once again she didn't know what she was trying to say. There was certainly tension building between them, and Kyle made her feel things and think things that no other man had; things that scared her, fascinated her, and yet at the same time repulsed her. Her own sensuality shocked her.

"I want you, Laura," he admitted. "I also know you want me, and it's not just my imagination." He took her hand and placed it over his heart. It was hammering full speed. Then he placed his hand over her heart, which was pounding just as hard.

"It's just lust," she suggested.

"I don't deny that I lust for you." He pressed her hand to the bulge between his legs, leaving no doubt about his claim. "I don't mean to shock you, but I'm not going to let you go until we've got things cleared up between us. You already know that I want you. I want to make love to you so badly I ache. But sex isn't all I want from you, Laura Davis. I apologize if I've left you with that impression. When I told you last night that I wanted to know you totally, I meant more than just physically."

That was what frightened her, Laura realized. It wasn't just having sex with Kyle that made her want to run scared; the truth of the matter was, she was afraid to give herself, to feel, to let herself go. She was afraid to fall in love. She'd been in love once, and it had hurt. She had pretended it didn't matter, but it did. She had felt destroyed when Nick had walked out on her.

Yet she was attracted to Kyle. She remembered how her body tingled when he looked at her. God, she was so confused.

"I can't, Kyle."

"Yes, you can, Laura. Believe me, the best way to deal with this is to meet it head-on."

"How?"

"Let it happen. Don't fight it."

Laura knew he wasn't talking about fear anymore. He was referring to them, to their relationship. "If that's how I'm supposed to handle it, I may as well let you take me right here, then," she said, "in the front seat of this car."

"Don't degrade it, either, Laura," he said forcefully,

"and think that by offending me you're going to make me angry enough to go away. We've already established that there's more than sex between us. You can't shut me out of your life; I won't let you. What we feel for each other is right and beautiful, and maybe we don't know exactly what it is yet, but it's real, whether we've known each other for three days or three years or three centuries."

"I'm just not sure, Kyle. I have so many doubts. I want you and I don't want you. I'm scared, and yet I'm practically throwing myself at you. I don't know you; I don't know me; I don't know what we're doing or why we're doing it." She sighed. "I don't even know why I let you kiss me last night."

"I accept your uncertainty. We can give it more time, if that's what you want. I can back off. It'll be hard, but that's nothing new. It's been a problem I've had to deal with since the moment I saw you seven months ago. But the bottom line is, I want you, and I'm willing to wait."

"For how long?"

"However long it takes."

He confused her, too, the way he was acting, so gentle and tender. Maybe she should let him make love to her, let their relationship develop, Laura thought. If only she didn't have these conflicting emotions, if only she knew how she would react.

Suddenly she needed to reaffirm to herself that she was an attractive woman. She needed to know that he found her desirable. "Will you kiss me, Kyle?"

He groaned. "I'd like very much to kiss you right now, Laura, but if I do, nothing on this earth could make me stop. I would end up taking you right here in the car."

"Will you take me home after the meeting, then?"

"Yes, if you want me to."

Someone knocked on the car window. "What are you two doing?" Phyllis called. "Solving the problems of the world? The meeting's supposed to be upstairs."

"Be right there," Kyle said. He turned back to Laura. "Are you all right?"

"Yes."

"We'll talk later. Okay?"

She nodded. "I think I need to concentrate on this operation instead of you."

He smiled and winked at her. "I'd be your partner no matter what you concentrated on, Laura."

"That, Agent Patterson," she said, hitching her purse over her shoulder, "scares me almost as much as you do."

He laughed and took her hand. "Let's go, Officer Davis. Enough soul-searching. It's time to get back to work."

CHAPTER SEVEN

JIM AND STAN ARRIVED at the Federal Building right behind Kyle and Laura. They took the same elevator up to the Bureau offices. When they had all grabbed a cup of coffee, Stan turned to her.

"That was good shooting this morning."

"Thanks," Laura answered.

"I don't know if anyone mentioned this to you, but I wasn't too thrilled with you being part of this detail. I know now that was a mistake on my part. You're damned good, and you deserve a chance."

Laura appreciated his compliments, but she knew she really didn't deserve them. All she'd done was beat everyone qualifying at the range. "I haven't done anything yet."

"You will," he answered. "We all will. We'll get these guys, Laura." He nodded, as though agreeing with himself. "We'll get them together. We're a good team."

Kyle called to them before Laura could respond. "Gather round, folks." He sat on the edge of a desk again. "Okay, let's hear it. Did anyone hit pay dirt?"

Unfortunately no one had any luck tracing down guns, either. Kyle's conversation with the pawnbroker was the most positive thing that had happened to any of them.

He glanced to the agent monitoring the phone. He was different from the one who had been there yesterday. Apparently they were taking shifts. The man sat with a mound of paperwork at his side, listening. "Anything?"

The agent shook his head.

"Keep me posted."

"Sure thing."

Kyle sighed. "I suppose we can't expect to sweep the city clear of crime in one day. Let's go home. We'll meet here tomorrow at the same time and hit the streets about midday. No sense getting out before the perps. Laura and I will take the west sector. The rest of you work what you had today."

"Still want us to avoid regular contacts?" Jim asked. "I can check with that hooker anytime."

"Thanks, but let's give it a couple days before we panic," Kyle answered. "Take it easy," he said, dismissing everyone. "Have a good night."

Except for the man monitoring the telephone, they all filed out of the room, laughing and chatting. Phyllis was headed for the health club, Sam a nearby bakery. Stan and Jim were riding together and were anxious to get home. No one seemed at all surprised that Laura hung back, waiting for Kyle. Phyllis turned and waved. So did Jim.

"Hang loose," he called.

Laura nodded. She should go, too. She should get on the elevator and go home, avoid Kyle Patterson. Even fools knew enough to stay away from fires. But before she could leave, Kyle took hold of her arm. "Hi. Ready?"

"For what?"

The moment she said the words she realized that she was going to have to keep a tighter rein on her mouth. But he smiled. "Feeling blunt tonight?"

She shrugged. "I guess."

"We could catch the sunset again."

She chewed her lip thoughtfully. "Kyle, I want off this operation."

"What?" He frowned at her.

"I want—"

"I heard you, Laura. I just don't understand you."

Sighing, she took a few steps away from him. Then she turned back to him. "I can't deal with being with you like this. I'm so confused. I'm not even concentrating on the detail."

"I told you I'd back off, Laura."

"That's not the answer, Kyle," she said. "It isn't even the problem, not really. I feel inadequate. I'm afraid I'm going to mess up."

"You're afraid of me, Laura, and more than that, you're afraid of failing." He shook his head. "I'm sorry, but since I'm in charge of this operation, I'm going to have to deny your request. I won't let you do this to yourself."

"I want out."

"No, you don't," he contradicted her. "You want assurance that everything is going to work out all right, that we're going to catch the people stealing these guns, that you aren't going to freeze up in a crisis situation.

You want guarantees, Laura, but there are no guarantees in police work, just like there are no guarantees in life."

When she didn't answer he moved closer to her, tilting her chin gently so that she was looking up at him. "Laura, you've got to prove it to yourself," he went on softly. "You've got to prove to Laura Davis that you're good enough. If I let you leave this operation, you'll never get another chance."

Although she knew he was right, Laura was still uncertain as she stared into his eyes. "Kyle, if I go to the boat with you tonight, you'll end up making love to me," she murmured. "You know it as well as I do."

He glanced toward the man monitoring the telephone. The guy was wearing radio headphones now, doing paperwork, and wasn't paying attention to them. "Not necessarily."

"I thought we were going to be honest with each other," she said. "Or were you just playing games with me in the car?"

"I don't play games."

"Neither do I."

"Well?"

He'd tossed the ball back in her corner. She studied him for a long moment. "You told me this morning I wasn't ready."

"You aren't."

"I want to be ready. How do I do that, Kyle?" Sometimes she surprised herself. "How do I get ready for making love with you?"

"I don't know, Laura." His expression was as serious as hers. "I wish I had the answer. I wish I had the answer for a lot of things. But we do have time. There's no need to rush. We can watch the sunset and see what happens."

She didn't want to see the sunset. She wanted to see the dawn. She wanted to take a chance on life and love again. "If I go to the boat with you, will you kiss me?"

"If you want me to. Look, I think you're carrying this honesty a little far. I told you this afternoon that I wouldn't push you. I meant that. We have the rest of our lives."

"Do you love me?"

Kyle seemed as stunned as Laura by her question. Being blunt was one thing, but this was quite another. Why in the world had she asked such a thing? It was just that she was feeling so off balance.

"I'm sorry," she said. "I'm not making sense."

"Yes, you are," he answered. "And you have every right to know what you're getting into. To be truthful, I don't know yet if I'm in love with you. I feel very deeply for you and I have for a long time. I told you that last night. But I don't know if it's love."

What is love anyhow but an elusive emotion between two people, Laura thought, a bond? Philosophers had tried to define it for centuries and as yet no one had been successful. Why was she trying to figure it out?

"Tell you what," Kyle suggested, "let's go watch the sunset from the park. That way you won't feel threatened. There'll be lots of people around, and you don't have to go near the boat. You can leave whenever you want."

Laura nodded. "I'd like that."

"Good." He took her hand. "Let's go."

They picked up chicken and trimmings at a fast-food restaurant and drove to the park that adjoined the harbor. As Kyle had promised, the place was crowded with people and cars. Laughing children ran through the grass, dogs barked, teenage couples held hands and giggled. While Laura fixed their plates at a picnic table, Kyle went to the boat for a blanket. After they ate, they spread the blanket under a tree and watched the sun disappear from the sky.

Even though darkness closed in, Laura felt comfortable being with him. He hadn't made a single move to touch her. Without thinking, she leaned her head against his shoulder as lights were turned on in the buildings, twinkling magically, much the same way as they had the night before. An occasional horn reminded her they were near the Outer Drive. As the night descended, people left the park, taking their dogs with them. And then, Kyle and Laura were alone.

"Cold?" he asked, rubbing her arm.

She had shivered. "A bit."

"Want my jacket?"

"I'll be fine." Laura knew she should move away, but she stayed in the protective circle of his arms. "Do you think you should check in to see if anyone has called about the guns?"

"My beeper's on."

"You're very laid back about police work, Kyle."

"Why do you say that?"

"You don't worry about when things are happening, what's happening, or *if* they're going to happen."

"It doesn't do any good to worry, Laura," he said, pulling her closer, but she didn't move away. "All we can do is wait and see."

"Is that how you feel about life, too?"

"Sometimes."

"How about love?"

He glanced down at her. "You seem to have an obsession about love."

She smiled. "Do I? I'm sorry. I have to confess, though, I have ulterior motives."

"Such as?"

Should she confess? "What I really want to know is how many women you've had."

He frowned. She could almost feel his puzzlement. "Why?"

"I'm curious," she admitted.

"Are you sure that's the real reason?"

"What else could there be?"

"Titillation."

"Oh, please!" Laura started to rise up in indignation, but Kyle pulled her back down.

"Don't get all upset. There's nothing wrong with titillation . . . in its place. Okay. I'll be honest with you. I've had a lot of experiences, but believe me, I'm just as afraid of this as you are."

Somehow she hadn't expected him to say that. "Really?"

"Really," he said slowly into her ear.

Laura wasn't certain how it happened but all of a sudden they weren't sitting on the blanket anymore. Kyle had lowered her gently to the ground, and she was staring up at him. She could see his face in the soft night and noticed the tiny scar at the edge of his temple, the creases in his forehead, and the laugh lines around his eyes. She could feel the warmth of his body next to hers, and she wanted to touch him, to place her hand on his chest and feel his heart beating next to hers.

"Kyle?" she murmured.

"Let's get that kiss out of the way, Laura."

Her breath stopped in her throat as she watched his

mouth close the gap between them. At first the kiss was gentle, his lips barely brushing across hers, like the time he'd kissed her on board the boat. Her heart felt like it was pounding a thousand miles an hour. Uncertainty fluttered in her belly. And longing.

Then, as he gathered her close and increased the pressure of his mouth on hers, sensations surged through her, and she moaned and arched against him. She couldn't think. All she could do was feel and yearn for more.

Yet Kyle was tender, his mouth caressing hers softly and gently. He trailed his hand down her jaw along her throat. His touch sent sparks throughout her; wherever he touched felt hot. She gasped when he cupped her breast and a blazing heat started in her belly.

"Oh, Kyle," she murmured. When he rubbed his thumb slowly across the nipple, she felt a quickening between her legs, a contracting sensation that made her quiver with need. "Oh, God, Kyle."

"Open your mouth, Laura," he said, and when she did, he darted his tongue inside the hot recess, exploring slowly, leisurely. All the while his thumb played with her nipple. Of its own volition her flesh peaked and strained against the soft fabric of her brassiere.

"Please," she murmured, not even knowing what she was pleading for.

"What, love?"

"I . . ."

Another gasp escaped her as he trailed his hand from her breast, down across her stomach, caressing, probing. Her skirt was hitched up around her thighs and his fingers slipped easily between her legs. She felt as though a hot brand had touched her. Fire raged inside her, the flames licking higher and higher, so intense she couldn't speak or breathe. Unconsciously she arched her hips against his fingers.

Then Kyle groaned and clutched her tightly to his body. His kisses became harsh, brutal, his mouth possessing hers, his tongue darting in and out.

"Laura," he cried hoarsely. "Oh, God, Laura, I can't hold back anymore."

Whether it was the intensity of his embrace that frightened her or rationality finally returning, Laura suddenly felt fear rush through her like a flood. "Please," she said, "don't." She pushed against his chest. "Kyle, stop."

It had to have been pure agony, but Kyle drew back. "What's wrong, Laura?"

She sat up, dragging her hands through her hair. God, they were in a park, petting, like a couple of teenagers. She was so ashamed. She'd known him for three days and she'd let him touch her intimately. "I can't, Kyle. This—this isn't right." Yet she knew she wanted him.

"What's not right?"

She drew a ragged breath. "This. Us. Kyle, I'm sorry. I can't do this."

At first he didn't say anything. She felt his silence envelop her like the night, dark, lonely, and empty. Finally he said softly, "No, I'm sorry, Laura. I should have controlled myself."

She shook her head. She couldn't let him blame himself. "This doesn't have anything to do with how you acted. It doesn't have anything to do with my having been raped."

That was a lie and she knew it. The terror she had felt had everything to do with her being raped, but she couldn't admit it, not to him, not even to herself, not just yet. She needed time—to adjust, to conquer her sense of shame and degradation, her fear.

"Laura?" When he touched her arm she had to steel herself not to cringe. "Are you sure? You reminded me earlier that we're supposed to be honest with each other. Remember?"

"I am being honest. I'm sorry, Kyle. I know I've led you on. There's a name for women like me, and it isn't very nice."

"It's called confused."

Moving away slightly, she tried to readjust her blouse and tuck it into her skirt, but her movements were jerky, ineffective. "Look, maybe you're right. Maybe I am old-fashioned."

She felt his gaze on her for the longest time. "Do you want me to say I love you?"

Laura paused, her hand still fumbling with the waistband of her skirt, and looked at him. He was staring at her so earnestly, so openly, this man who had come into her life and made her feel things she didn't want to acknowledge.

"Do you want me to say I love you?" he repeated.

She turned away. She didn't want him to say anything he didn't feel, but oh, God, how she wished he felt it. "Look, I have to go."

"Laura, please." He reached for her hand.

"Don't touch me!" Out of habit she jerked away. "God, I'm sorry," she said moments later. When would she stop overreacting to a man's touch? "Kyle, please understand, you haven't done anything wrong, but I need to go home. I need to get away from you for a while."

"All right," he answered softly. "I understand. I'll take you."

"No, I'll get a cab."

"I'll drive you. I insist."

She felt as if she were going to explode. "No," she said, balling her hands into fists. "Don't you see? If you take me home you'll want to kiss me good-night. You'll want to talk. You won't be satisfied with letting me alone. I can't face that, Kyle. Please, please," she begged, "give me some space. Don't push me."

Once again the silence stretched between them. "Will you be all right?"

She nodded. "I'll be fine."

If he didn't like her answer, at least he seemed to accept it. "Wait here," he said. "I'll flag down a cab for you."

The street was just a few yards away through the trees. After he walked away, Laura stood, still feeling shaky, and brushed off her clothes. Why couldn't she just let go, Laura thought? What they were feeling for each other was natural and beautiful. She had behaved like the teenage girl who was running through the parking lot, letting the young boy chase her and catch her, and then running away again. But Laura knew she couldn't act any differently even if she wanted to. No matter how hard she tried, she couldn't control her fear. Whether she liked it or not, her reaction to Kyle Patterson scared her.

To his credit Kyle didn't try to touch her or dissuade her as he tucked her inside the cab and gave the driver her address. He leaned through the window. "See you tomorrow. I'll pick you up around ten. Get some sleep."

"Sure."

All the way home Laura tried very hard not to think about what had happened between her and Kyle, and what *might* have happened between them had she let it.

Unfortunately she wasn't very successful. By the time she unlocked her front door, she was more upset than she had been in the park. Her stomach churned with unresolved emotions, questions, and agony.

Why had she turned away from him? Why couldn't she let go and let him make love to her? Good God, he'd only kissed her and she'd acted like he'd attacked her. The man was everything a woman would want: kind, patient, sexy. When he looked at her she felt beautiful, special.

No, that wasn't the entire truth. Whenever Kyle Patterson looked at her, Laura felt consumed by yearning. She wanted him to take her and make mad, passionate love to her. She wanted him to ignore her objections and kiss her until she couldn't object any more. She wanted him to touch her, to make her feel, to make her forget.

And that, more than anything, frightened her.

Her hands trembled so that she could hardly turn the key. Damn! She pushed open the door and stepped into the vestibule. A huge, hairy spider brushed against her face. Not realizing it was fake, she gasped and batted at the thing until it jerked off of its string and fell onto the floor, upside down.

Laura stared at the spider while her heart resumed normal speed, and she caught her breath. The thing was rubber, and it had scared her to death. Drawing a deep sigh, she picked it up and turned it over in her palm. It was bumpy, with grotesque red and green streaks running down the eight hairy legs. "Kevin, you little devil," she muttered. "If you keep up this mischief, your mother's going to punish you for eternity."

Shaking her head, she pocketed the toy spider and went on up the steps. The kid wasn't the only one playing tricks, Laura admitted to herself. She was playing tricks, too, with Kyle, teasing him one moment, backing away the next. But what could she do about it, punish herself?

In a way that was what she was doing by denying her feelings, by running away from him. Dr. Lowenstein would be furious with her. "You have to stop sticking your head in the sand, Laura," the therapist would say. "This problem exists. Confront it."

She sighed. If she wasn't careful she was going to make a career of sighing. Why couldn't she think and decide what she wanted? Her gaze fell on Cassie's note; perhaps talking to a friend would help.

Frustrated, she picked up the phone and dialed her friend's number. Cassie answered on the first ring. It was then that Laura remembered that her friend was supposed to have had a date that night with the construction worker.

"Are you alone?" she asked.

There was a brief pause. Soft music played in the background. Had she interrupted something important? "I can be. Is something wrong?"

"I need to talk."

There was not a single moment's hesitation in Cassie's answer. "I'll be right there."

True to her word, Cassie arrived less than a half hour later, sweeping up the steps with a broad smile.

"God, Laura," she said the moment she'd tossed down her purse, "the man is a hunk."

"I gather your date was nice."

"My date was wonderful," Cassie corrected. "I think this is it—the real thing."

"He lights your fire?"

"Laura, this guy not only lights my fire, he sends sparks up my chimney."

Laura laughed. "That good, huh?"

"Sexually? Actually I wouldn't know," Cassie answered. "He respects me and he wants to wait. Lord, I love it." She stared at Laura. "I gather Kyle Patterson's trying to build a bonfire under you, and you've run for the water hoses."

"Do you ever mince words, Cassie?"

"Nope. What happened?"

"Nothing."

"You're pretty upset about nothing."

Laura started to pace the floor. "Want something to drink?"

"It's nearly midnight."

"Do you turn into a pumpkin?"

"That's an old joke."

"I know." Laura flopped in a chair. "I'm not going to sigh."

"Okay."

Laura looked out the windows at the night. "I'm repressing my feelings again."

"Is that bad?"

"Yes."

"What would Dr. Lowenstein say?"

Laura shrugged. "I'm sick of thinking about what Dr. Lowenstein would say. The woman's giving me a headache, and I haven't even seen her in weeks."

"Maybe you should see her," Cassie said. "It might help. I think you're giving yourself the headache, though. What's the matter?"

"Kyle Patterson lights my fire."

Cassie arched an eyebrow in surprise. "Oh. That's kind of nice."

"Is it?" Laura glanced at her friend. "I've only known him for three days."

"So?"

"So how can you fall in love in three days?"

"Easy. People do it all the time. Bam, you're in love."

"Who?"

"How do I know who? People. Me for one. I'm in love, and it's only been one day. Cleopatra, too, I think," she said. "She fell in love with Marc Antony in three days or something like that. Maybe even at first sight."

"How can I be in love when I can't even stand being touched by a man?" Laura remarked.

"Oh, hell, Laura, you've been raped. How do you expect to react to a man?"

"I don't know how I *expect* to react to a man," Laura said, "but I *want* to react like a normal woman."

Cassie studied her for a few moments. "Then go for it."

Laura met her friend's steady gaze. "I'm scared."

"So?"

"You're just full of sympathy tonight, aren't you?"

"Hey, I don't mean to take anything away from you," Cassie said in her own defense. "I know you've been raped, and I can imagine that it was hell, but why are you letting it ruin your life? You've got to get back on the horse eventually."

"Oh, God, I don't believe you're using that old cliché," Laura answered. "I'm sorry, Cassie, but being raped isn't like riding a horse. I'm not going to get laid just to prove to myself that I can do it."

"Why not?" As usual her friend was blunt, and not at all put off by Laura's anger. "If you want to get on with your life, you've got to start living again. Nobody else can do it for you."

Laura went back to staring out the window.

"Of course, it's up to you," Cassie went on. "You can spend your life hiding from men and from relationships or you can go for it. Maybe you just need some more time, Laura." She stood and picked up her purse. "Hey, I've got to go. I've got to be present for roll call at seven, and you know how long it takes me to get ready for work. If you're asking my advice, I'd say you're a fool to let him get away. Then again, you could give yourself a few days. You're getting back on track with your career. You've transferred to this operation, and you're apparently doing a good job. Maybe your personal life will shape up, too. And if you're not asking my advice," she concluded, "ignore me."

With that, Cassie walked out the door. After her friend left, Laura sat in the chair sulking. What was she going to do? Cassie was right, her career was getting back on track, but she'd had to fight for it. She'd had to convince Kyle that she was ready. Hell, she'd had to convince herself that she was ready.

Absently Laura picked up the rubber spider and turned it over, studying the hairy legs. The thing was supposed to be scary but in reality it was not. She sat up, staring at the thing. It was really nothing. Suddenly she tossed it aside and grabbed a sweater. Why hadn't she realized it before? Her fear was nothing, too, because it could be conquered. It couldn't possess her unless she let it.

What a fool she'd been. If she wanted any chance at all at a normal life, at a husband and children and yes, love, she had to meet this crisis head-on. She'd known that all along; she'd just been avoiding the pain. She was going to go to Kyle and face him, like a woman goes to a man, and this time she wasn't going to run away. She could only hope that he would let her in.

Her course decided, she rushed down the steps. Just before she opened the door downstairs, she hurried back up and grabbed three pieces of candy, attaching them to the string that had held the spider, one for each of the three children.

CHAPTER EIGHT

How did you knock on a boat?

Clutching a brown paper bag in her hands, Laura stared at the long, sleek craft bobbing up and down in the water. There wasn't a door, and there certainly wasn't a doorbell. It was late so she didn't want to call to Kyle and wake up the entire harbor. The silence was eerie. The only sound she could hear was water lapping against the side of the pier. Everything along the dock was dark, including his cabin. What if he wasn't there? What if he had left to find another woman, someone who wouldn't just tease him, who would respond to his kisses, caresses, who would kiss him back and touch him, love him?

She was chickening out again, Laura realized, looking for excuses to allow her to go back home, and it disgusted her. She'd never been a coward before. *She'd never gone to a man with the express purpose of making love before, either.*

"Kyle," she called softly, leaning over the narrow gap of water between the boat and the dock, and tapping on the dark hull. "Kyle, are you home?"

More silence.

She knocked again. "Kyle?"

Suddenly, he came through the doorway, hurriedly snapping his pants. "Laura, is that you?"

"Hi," she said, trying to smile. She felt shy, strangely reticent. But then she stared into his eyes and lost herself in the intensity of his gaze. Lord, but he was sexy, standing there barefoot and barechested. His chest was hairy and his hair was mussed. He'd been sleeping, and the thought of him naked in his bunk sent feelings of longing and need rushing through her, making her heart beat faster and her breathing falter.

"Hi, yourself," he answered in a husky tone. "What's up?"

What would he look like naked in bed? Gorgeous, sexy, his body would be hard, firm, the muscles taut. Laura closed her eyes to make the image go away. Taking a deep, calming breath, she gestured around at the boats. "Everybody's asleep."

He nodded. "It's late. How did you get here?"

Had she made a mistake in coming? Chewing her lips nervously she said, "I took a cab."

"You should have called."

"You have a phone?"

"Yes."

"Oh," she said, forcing another smile. Why was she so nervous? "I didn't know that. I didn't notice it when I was here before."

"It's on the wall," he answered. "You shouldn't be out alone at night, Laura. It's dangerous."

"Chicago has lots of cops."

The joke fell flat. She cleared her throat. Why wasn't he saying anything, doing anything? She'd thought he'd be happy to see her, but he just stood there staring at her.

"I thought you said the harbor was different."

"It's not that different."

Okay, now what? Even though his gaze was enough to send shivers down her spine, asking, "Do you want to make love to me?" seemed a bit outspoken, although she had certainly been brazen with him in the past. She glanced around again. "Aren't you going to invite me aboard?"

"No."

She hadn't expected that answer. "Why not?"

He didn't respond to her question. "Wait a minute. I'll get my car keys and take you back home."

"I don't want to go home," she said sharply, making him pause.

He stared at her. "Then what is it you do want, Laura?"

She tossed him the bag she'd been holding. He caught it, frowning at it as she explained. "I stopped at a drugstore on the way over here."

"And?"

"And I bought something." She took a deep breath. This was what she wanted. "Maybe you ought to take a look at it."

He opened the bag, all the while glancing from it to her as though he thought she might have lost her mind. "What is it?"

"Some green stuff," she said with a shrug as he

pulled out the can of slime. "It seemed to be kind of effective the last time we were together."

"Effective?" he repeated softly. "Tell me, Laura, what are you suggesting we do with it?"

"Rub it on each other?"

He was amazed at her suggestion; she could tell by the way he looked at her. "Laura, you have some interesting ideas for a woman who's inhibited."

"I'm not inhibited," she said. "And despite what you think or what I said earlier, I'm not even old-fashioned." She glanced at her watch. "Now that it's past midnight, I've known you for four whole days. And if you count that time you were here before, it's been months."

"So?"

"It's a long time, don't you think?"

"Depends."

"Look." She gestured at the boat. "Isn't it kind of silly for me to be standing here on shore and for you to be standing there on that boat when we could both be standing there together?"

The small craft bobbed up and down while he contemplated her words. "Laura, if I let you come on board this boat, I won't be able to keep my hands off you. We'll end up making love."

"I know." She swallowed the lump of apprehension in her throat. "I was hoping you'd have that problem."

"Pardon me?" It was almost as if he couldn't believe what he had heard.

"I was hoping you'd have that problem," she repeated loudly.

"Shh." Frowning, he glanced around at the other boats. "You don't have to wake everybody up."

"Then listen to me."

He arched an eyebrow at her. "Point taken. Okay, let me get this straight. You're here, and you know that if you stay we're going to make love?"

"Uh-huh."

"You're sure that's what you want?"

"I can hardly wait."

She stood still, her stomach churning, while he studied her. "Damn," he muttered. "Come on, Laura." He held out his hand. "I think we better make some coffee."

She smiled and clasped his hand, hopping across the narrow schism of water. Since he didn't move back, she brushed against his body, her breasts rubbing his chest. "What happened to the apple cider you fixed the other night?"

"I need the caffeine," he answered. "I have a feeling this is going to be a long night."

The words sounded ominous, and not at all sensual. Laura followed him into the cabin. She'd guessed right. He had been sleeping. Or lying in bed at least. The covers were rumpled.

She sat in the same chair she'd occupied the last time she'd been there and watched him move around the small galley. He was tall and broad-shouldered, but he seemed comfortable in these small surroundings. He had put on a shirt and run his hands through his hair. He looked sexy.

"Okay," he said when he'd fixed the coffeepot and placed it on the stove. He grabbed the cream and sugar and slammed them on the table as he sat down across from her. "Maybe you better tell me what's going on."

Why was he being so suspicious? She'd already told him what she wanted. "I—"

"The truth," he cut in.

Laura flushed. "I did tell you the truth."

"Refresh my memory," he said.

"I want you to make love to me."

"Just like that?"

Why was he making it so difficult for her? "Any way you want, actually."

Once more her attempt at humor fell short. With an almost angry glare at her, he stood up and started to unbutton his shirt. His movements were harsh and jerky.

"What are you doing?" she asked.

"Getting ready."

She stared at him in dread. Why was he being deliberately cruel, treating their attraction as though it were just an encounter? But she'd treated it that way, too, hadn't she, by coming here and asking him to make love to her. Maybe that was why he was angry.

"Get up," he said.

"Kyle, please," she murmured.

"You said you'd do it any way I wanted it, Laura. What's the matter? Change your mind again?"

What was she going to do now? But she'd come here for a reason, and she wasn't about to back out. She stood up. "No, I haven't changed my mind."

Apparently he hadn't expected that answer. He scowled at her. "Sit down."

She did, in relief, but she said, "I wish you'd make up your mind."

That made him laugh. He chuckled, loud and long. "God, I love you," he said.

"Pardon me?"

"I love you. Is that so surprising?"

Laura sat with her mouth open as he put the coffee on the table and turned up the lanterns. The room took on a brilliant glow.

"What are you doing now?" she asked.

"Getting ready," he answered, but this time the words were husky, sexy, touching her like a caress. "I want to see every inch of you when I make love to you."

"Oh."

"Oh, is right." He leaned against the counter, legs spread wide, and studied her, his eyes caressing her soft curves much as his voice had caressed her soul moments ago. "Come here, Laura."

She couldn't have disobeyed his command any more than she could have stopped her heart from beating. Kyle was going to make love to her. She knew it as surely as she was breathing. He would make her feel again, he would make her whole. They would find love together.

Mesmerized by his gaze, she walked slowly toward him, stopping only when her body brushed his. She licked her lips in the one sign of nervousness she allowed to show as he pressed her hips against his thighs. She could feel his arousal, hard against her softness, but she refused to succumb to fear. He would be gentle. And if he wasn't, this was still what she wanted.

"I'm here," she said softly. "What do you want me to do?"

"Nothing," he murmured hoarsely, as though he were having trouble breathing, too. "Just stand here and let me look at you." He touched her cheek. "I want to feel you. You're so soft, Laura, so beautiful. I love you. I don't know how it happened or when, but I love you. I think I've loved you since the day I met you."

"I love you, Kyle," she whispered, returning the words.

"I don't need to hear it, Laura."

"But it's true," she said, surprised to realize she was speaking the truth. "I do love you."

When had it happened? When had she fallen in love? Had it been love all along between them and not lust? Yet she lusted for him and he for her. The hardness she felt pressing between her legs attested to that, as did the fire that licked at her belly.

"I'm glad." Kyle trailed his hand down her cheek and along the smooth column of her throat, pausing at the buttons of her blouse. "Ready?"

"Just like that?" she remarked.

"Do you want me to do something?"

"No."

"Do you want to talk?"

"No."

"Afraid?"

"A bit."

Slowly he started to undo the buttons, one by one. "It's all right to be afraid. I told you earlier that I was afraid, too."

"I know."

"How many men have you been with, Laura?"

The question startled her.

"Why?"

"Curiosity."

"Is that all?"

"Indulge me. How many men have you been with?"

"A few."

"Nick?"

"Yes."

"Before?"

She knew he meant before the rape. "Yes."

"Who else?"

"A guy in college."

"And Calimara."

She shivered. "Yes."

"Damn." Kyle muttered.

"It's all right," she said. "I'm over it."

"Maybe." She knew he didn't believe her. She didn't believe herself. "The man is crud, and I'll always regret not being able to help you that night."

"It's all right. I understand." Kyle was undoing the last of the buttons. Her blouse was almost open, her body exposed, like her fears.

"I don't." Yet he went on, softly, probing. "With the others, were you satisfied? Did you climax?"

"Why are you doing this?" she asked. "Why are you asking me these things?"

"Trust me, Laura." He paused. "Did you climax?"

"God." Yet she did trust him. "Yes. A few times."

"Was it good?"

"Yes." She shivered again as he slid the blouse off her shoulders, and the cool night air caressed her skin.

"Did you enjoy it?"

"Yes," she whispered in an agonized tone. "Yes, I enjoyed it."

"Good."

As though fearful of touching her, he traced a finger lightly along the lacy edge of her bra. Her breasts strained against the garment, and when he released them they surged forward. Laura had never been naked before like this, in front of a man with blazing lights, and at first, she wanted to hide her nakedness. She crossed her arms in front of her breasts.

"No, don't," he said, brushing her hands away. "Let me look at you."

She felt uncomfortable as his gaze traveled over her body, and yet at the same time, desire raged through her. She begged silently for his touch, but he kept his hands at his sides.

"Are you still sure this is what you want?"

"Yes."

"Are you still afraid?" he probed again.

"No."

Why couldn't he just get on with it? She leaned against him, but he pushed her away from his thighs, letting her skirt fall into a pool at her feet. She hadn't realized that he had already unzipped the garment. He tugged at her slip and panties, sliding them down her legs. "Lift your feet, Laura."

When she did as he asked, he tossed the garments out of their way and simply looked at her, stared at her almost reverently.

"Kyle?"

"God, you're beautiful."

"Please."

"Please what?"

"Don't stop."

With a groan of pleasure, he closed his eyes as he rested her back against his hardness. But still he didn't touch her. She swayed toward him, needing him, wanting him.

"Kyle—"

"Wait, Laura." Groaning again, he moved slightly, adjusting her. "Go easy, babe."

So he was having problems maintaining control. She smiled at that knowledge. "I don't want to go easy."

"I do," he answered almost gruffly. "Wait," he commanded again, gritting his teeth in near agony. Then, when he'd managed to start breathing normally again, he looked at her and pulled the pins from her hair, letting it down strand by strand. "You have lovely hair." He stroked his hands through it. "So long and silky."

"Thank you."

"Soft. You're soft all over," he went on, placing his hands on her shoulders and running them down her arms, across her stomach, up to her breasts, softly stroking the darkened areola that surrounded her nipples. "So beautiful."

"Kyle?"

She shivered again, this time from arousal as he cupped the naked flesh in his hands and licked the nipples with his tongue. Taking the peaks in his mouth, he suckled gently, first one and then the other. Laura's breathing grew ragged, and she slumped against him, her legs refusing to hold her any longer.

"Oh, God, Laura," he murmured, setting her gently away. "Let me get my pants off."

Laura felt her heart pound and her hands sweat as she waited for him to shrug out of his pants and shorts. What would she do when she saw his nakedness? Would she feel threatened by it? She closed her eyes and commanded her feet not to move. She wasn't going to run away, not again.

"Laura?" he called her name softly. "Look at me, Laura."

She couldn't.

"Open your eyes."

Slowly she opened them, but she kept her gaze riveted to his face. She tried to smile. "Hi."

Not at all dissuaded by her ruse, Kyle took her hand. "Touch me, Laura."

Although she swallowed hard, she did as he commanded, closing her fingers around his turgid length. At her touch, he nearly choked with need.

"Man," he breathed and for a moment, he couldn't speak. With a ragged sigh, he said, "Look at me, Laura. Now."

She didn't understand his point in going through all this, but she knew he was doing it for her benefit. Perhaps he felt it would help her. He knew she was afraid. No matter what she'd said, she was still petrified to let him make love to her. Gradually, obeying his request, she shifted her gaze down to her hand. Kyle's flesh filled her palm, warm and strong. She couldn't prevent the shiver of fear that rippled through her.

"Tell me about it, Laura," he said softly. "Tell me about the rape. Talk to me."

The mere thought of telling him about her violation made her panic. She couldn't do it. She couldn't talk to anyone about it. He should have known! Why had he asked?

"Talk to me, Laura."

"No, I can't!" She started to pull away from him but he grasped her wrist and pulled her back.

"Oh, no, Laura, not now," he said firmly. "I won't let you go now. We've come too far." In a softer tone he added, "I won't hurt you. I promise."

She wasn't certain she believed him, not that he would hurt her purposely, she knew that, but fear had crept in and she couldn't thrust it away. Forcing herself, she stood still, quivering again as he pulled her against his hips in much the same way as he had before. Only now his stiffness invaded her, sheathed within her nakedness.

"You need to touch me, Laura, to know me." He stroked her hair gently, quieting her. "Now, we're both naked, stripped bare. There are no secrets between us, nothing to make us fear each other. We have no reason to hold back. You've got to talk to me."

"What—what do you want me to say?"

"Tell me about the rape."

"It was awful."

"What did he do?"

"He ripped my dress."

"And?"

"Why are you doing this?" she cried. "You heard. You listened."

He held her firmly. "I'm sorry, Laura. I didn't mean to listen." But he didn't back off. "What did he do?"

"He touched me."

Kyle caressed her breasts. "Here?"

"Yes."

"Here?" He touched her intimately.

"No."

"What did he do?"

"He just threw me on the sofa and—and did it," she said, sickened at the memory. "God, I hate him."

Kyle caressed her hair again. "There's nothing to be afraid of now," he went on, stroking her gently. "I won't hurt you, and I won't let anyone else hurt you, either."

"I wanted to die," she said, letting the feelings out at last. "I felt so ashamed, like I had done something wrong."

"It wasn't your fault."

"I know." She looked up at him. "I felt ashamed anyhow."

"Do you still feel ashamed?"

"No," she said honestly. "Sometimes I don't feel anything at all, except anger. And fear."

"How about desire?"

Apparently he wasn't going to leave a single question unasked. "I feel desire," she admitted. "I've felt it a lot lately."

"For me?"

"Yes."

He touched her breast again, trailing his finger lightly around one nipple. "It doesn't have to hurt, Laura." He kept stroking his thumb back and forth across the peak. "Does this feel good?"

"Oh, God," she murmured as desire contracted her stomach. "Yes," she said at last, knowing he wanted an answer.

Dipping his dark head down, he pressed her breasts together and kissed the valley between them, cupping, licking, lolling his tongue around the peaks. Laura felt the flames in her belly start to sizzle and burn. She wanted this man with every fiber of her being.

"Kyle," she murmured again.

"Yes, love?"

"I—" She could hardly speak.

"What do you want, Laura? Tell me."

God, he liked to talk. "Kiss me. Make love to me."

Without further urging, he moved his mouth over hers in a passionate embrace. Still he was gentle, moving his lips back and forth, barely touching hers. Laura could hardly stand it. The moments seemed like hours as he continued to draw out the embrace. Whether it was purposeful or not, he moved his hips ever so slightly, sliding back and forth in her moist warmth, yet not penetrating, not satisfying. She felt tense, on edge, as if she were going to explode with need. She wrapped her hands around his neck, trying to pull him closer.

"Kyle," she murmured. "I can't stand it. I can't wait."

"You're sure?"

"Yes! Yes. Yes. Please, do it. Please make love to me."

His breath was coming fast, too, hot on her skin. He trailed his finger down her cheek and along her throat to the soft rise of her breast. "I might not be gentle, Laura. I might not be able to hold back."

"I—I don't want gentleness." She wanted the sensuality of the way he had kissed her the other night, the rough, hard feel of him next to her, inside of her. She wanted his hands on her body, touching her. She wanted him to possess her. Now, this moment.

"This is one hell of a responsibility, Laura. You could end up hating me."

"I could never hate you, Kyle."

"Laura?"

"Don't talk." She pressed her hips against him purposefully. "No more talk."

"All right, Laura. No more talk." He held her tightly. "You're right. It's time for action."

They were still standing up, leaning against a counter. All it took was a slight adjustment on her part, and he plunged inside her. She gasped at the shock of it as he filled her, and she slumped her head against his shoulder as pleasure coursed through her veins; intense, burning pleasure. He paused, too, for a moment; waiting, throbbing, swelling inside of her. Then he started to slowly move in and out.

Laura thought surely she was going to faint from the intensity of her feelings. The storm she had felt in his arms the first time he'd touched her returned to ravage her, and she wanted the wind to take her, to possess her. The emotions coursing through her were exhilarating, sweet and wild, like a blazing tempest. She cried out once as rapture claimed her, and her breath came in short gasps as he drew it out, until she crested the eye of the storm and her body jerked in spasms of pleasure.

At the height of her passion, Kyle cried out, too, and clutched her close as his own body jerked convulsively. "Oh, God, Laura."

He held her in his arms while they both came back to earth. It was a wonder to her that they were still standing. Her legs and arms were trembling, and if he hadn't been holding her she would have slid to the floor. Gradually her breathing slowed and her heart stopped flip-flopping around. She leaned her head against his chest.

Kyle expelled a long, telling sigh. "That was pretty damned good for a woman who's inhibited."

She was grateful for his compliment, even though it had been tossed out in an offhand manner. She had enjoyed their lovemaking, but she had felt unsure of herself, not knowing if she had pleasured him. "I've told you over and over that I'm not inhibited," she said, smiling up at him. "What more do I have to do to prove it?"

Reaching for the can of slime he'd placed on the counter, he lifted it suggestively and arched an eyebrow at her. "Put it to the test?"

She laughed. "Now?"

He backed her toward his bed. "Laura, love," he said huskily, "there's no better time."

Something woke Laura, maybe a boat horn in the distance, perhaps the water lapping on the side of the boat. She opened her eyes and saw Kyle. He was awake, too, staring at her as though he'd been memorizing her features. They had made love most of the night yet she didn't feel tired. She felt exhilarated. He had held her and caressed her until the memory of the rape had faded from her consciousness. It occurred to Laura that their relationship, though admittedly brief, had many levels. They went from intense sexuality to easy camaraderie, from silly to serious, from tough to gentle. They could talk about anything, she could tell him things she had never before told any human being. She could laugh with him, cry with him, talk with him, and not worry about embarrassing herself.

Dr. Lowenstein would be proud. "You've faced this well, Laura," she would say. "Making love with a man."

Kyle's touch felt as familiar as her skin. With his hands and lips he had stroked her body, discovering things about her that she didn't know herself. She felt as though she'd known him forever.

"Good morning," he said, leaning down to kiss her lips.

"Morning."

"Happy?"

"Very," she said, smiling. "You're pretty good at this, you know."

He laughed. "I've had lots of practice."

She stuck her tongue out at him. "Braggart. You know, if we keep this up, one of us is going to have to compromise."

"Why's that?"

"Your legs are scratchy."

He laughed. "Want me to buy pajamas?"

"Actually, it's something else that bothers me," she whispered, reaching to stroke him lightly. When he grew hard in her hands, she curled her fingers around him, moving back and forth in a rhythmic motion.

"Laura, we'll never get any sleep if we keep this up."

"Unfortunately I understand that after a while the novelty wears off."

"Are you sure?" He groaned and turned over. "I don't think I'll ever get tired of this."

"It shows."

"Be glad, woman."

"I am."

Kyle shifted, and unconsciously she licked her lips. "My God, Laura," he said, "you have the most fascinating mouth."

"Oh?"

"It could do some interesting things."

"Really? Like what?"

He pressed his hard length against her. "I'd be glad to show you."

"I'll just bet you would." She smiled and knelt above him. "But how about if I show you, instead?"

He sucked his breath inward. "Help yourself, ma'am."

Later, Laura rested her head on his chest, rubbing her fingers through the hairs absently. Each time they had made love, she reached new and higher heights of ecstasy. This last time had been like a raging wildfire.

Kyle kissed her. "You know, we never did have that coffee. Feel like breakfast?"

Realizing that she was hungry she glanced out the porthole just above their heads. The sky looked gray. "What time is it?"

"Dawn."

She'd wanted to see it with him, then she realized that in a way she had. "Surrender," she murmured softly.

"What?" Kyle said.

"Surrender the dawn." She glanced at him. "Haven't you ever heard that expression?"

He shook his head. "No. I thought the expression was dark before dawn."

"There's that one also," she said. "My father used to say 'Surrender the dawn.' I never understood its meaning until now."

"Which is?"

She looked at him as she kept running her hand over his bare chest. The hairs prickled sensuously, like they had that first time she'd touched him. "It means time for renewal. A new day is beginning, the dawn of your life. Surrender, and bask in its sunshine."

"That's beautiful."

"Yes, it is," she agreed. "I just hope it's true."

"You'll do fine on the operation, Laura," he said, apparently sensing her fears. "We're not going to let it go wrong."

"Can we do that, Kyle?"

"I believe we can do anything we set out to do. Together we can't miss."

She glanced out the porthole again as the sky began to grow light. She hoped he was right, because in a way, the entire operation could hinge on that statement. Although she was confident of herself as a woman now, she had yet to put herself to the test on the streets.

And that was the most terrifying test of all.

CHAPTER NINE

LAURA'S STREET TEST came sooner than she anticipated. They had just finished eating breakfast when Kyle's beeper went off. The call was so unexpected that Laura jumped and stared at the small, electronic device as though it were a snake in the grass.

Since Kyle was in the shower, and she didn't want to call the man monitoring the phone, implicitly announcing that she had spent the night with the boss, she went to the bathroom door and knocked softly. "Better hurry. It looks like we may have our fish."

"Did the beeper go off?" Kyle shut off the water.

"Loud and clear."

He opened the bathroom door and stepped out with a towel wrapped around his hips. He dripped water all over the floor; it ran off his legs in rivulets and dripped from his dark hair. "Did you call in?"

"No, I thought you'd better answer."

He arched an eyebrow at her as he headed for the telephone. "Don't want anyone to know?"

"It's not that, exactly."

"What is it, exactly?" he asked.

She shrugged. "I just don't normally flaunt my sex life."

Although his glance was skeptical, Kyle didn't answer. Holding up one finger to alert her to the fact that the subject wasn't closed, he picked up the phone and punched out the number of the Bureau. "You heard from somebody?" he said to the person on the other end. "What's going down?"

Laura waited with baited breath, listening to Kyle talk. This was so soon to have made the connection. It could be nothing, a false alarm. Or if it was something, it might not even be remotely connected to their goal, a shipload of Uzis. But Kyle turned to her as he talked, smiling broadly and nodding.

"Okay," he said to the man after a few moments. "Sounds good. Alert the team. I'll meet everybody at the central police station in thirty minutes, and we'll decide who goes. We have to be careful. This might be just a trial run. That pawnshop owner acted suspicious. Could be they're trying to see if we're legitimate or if we're cops, and we sure don't want to tip our hand."

"Did we get a buy?" Laura asked after he hung up.

"Maybe. Somebody's looking to unload a submachine gun."

"An Uzi?"

"Didn't say."

"Is it worth it?" What was one gun compared to the arsenal they were looking for?

"We can always hope there's more, and that they're the right product. If nothing else, we have to pretend. If we were revolutionaries we'd be interested in a single bullet."

"I suppose," Laura agreed.

"By the way, I thought we had decided we had more going for us than a sexual relationship."

Laura felt a stab of regret at the hurt look in his eyes. "I'm sorry, Kyle. I didn't mean that the way it sounded. I just didn't think it was wise to let the entire team know what had happened between us."

"Aren't you proud of it?"

What an odd way to phrase it. "Making love with a man is not something I can be proud of, Kyle, like a degree or an accomplishment. It's something that happened."

"I disagree. Love *is* an accomplishment, Laura. And making love is an expression of it."

She started to pace the floor. How could she explain her position? Her doubts? "Kyle, we don't know each other very well. We've just—"

"I know you well enough to realize that I want to spend the rest of my life with you," he said quietly. "What I don't know about you I can find out through the years."

"Are you—" She frowned. "Are you asking me to marry you?"

"Will you?"

"I don't know." She was suddenly nervous. Their relationship had moved forward so quickly. Although she was certain that she loved him, she still couldn't believe she had found the real thing. "I—I hadn't given it any consideration."

"What's to consider?"

"Where would we live, for one?"

"Your place. Or we could look for an apartment. We

could spend the summers here, on the boat."

"I can't sail."

He laughed. "I'll teach you."

Why was she so panic-stricken all of a sudden? The thought of making a lifetime commitment was almost as bad as the thought of sex a few hours ago. But that had worked out all right. "What would we do about our jobs? You're an agent for ATF and I'm a cop."

"We've managed so far, haven't we?"

"This is different. We can't be partners forever."

"People make compromises all the time, Laura," he said. "In their jobs, in their habits, in their lives. At least we're both on the same side."

"Kyle, I—"

"Look," he cut in, moving close to her and stroking her cheek lightly. "I know this is all strange and new to you. I don't mean to rush you. God knows, you're just getting yourself together, and I usually go slow, too, but please remember that I love you, Laura. I want to tell everybody I know that I love you."

"Stan?"

"Stan's in your corner these days."

"Only because I can shoot."

"Reason enough."

"What if I mess up, Kyle?"

"Shh, Laura," he said, "don't think that way. You're not going to mess up. I'll be there. I'll be beside you."

"Forever?"

His smile was tender as he tucked her hair back behind her ear. "Believe me, Laura, it's just going to take one arrest to get your confidence back."

Was that all it was, a matter of self-confidence? Perhaps he was right. She'd fought for this operation, but deep down inside she wasn't at all certain she was ready for it.

"And this might be it," he went on, winking at her. "What do you say, let's get going?"

He was so good to her, and now it was her turn to smile. "Thanks." She kissed him, lightly. "But don't you think you need to get dressed?"

He'd been standing in his towel. A tiny pool of water surrounded his feet. He looked down and laughed. "An excellent suggestion, Officer Davis. Turn your back."

"What?" Laura paused. "Are you saying you're shy?"

"Why is that so surprising?"

"After last night?"

"Making love is one thing, Laura, and getting dressed is quite another. Besides, I never could figure out how to look sexy while putting on socks."

"You'd look sexy putting in your dentures, Kyle Patterson," she said, but turned her back anyway. "If you had them. So don't worry about your socks."

When they got to the central police station Kyle decided that since the call seemed to be a test of sorts, just he and Laura would meet the pawnbroker. Everyone else would be in cars, ready to close in if there were any problems.

"Go get wired," he said to her when the team had agreed the decision seemed the most logical. "I'll be right there."

"Are you going to wear a microphone, too?"

He nodded. "Just in case we get separated."

"Don't you think that's risky? I'd bet the people we're meeting will try to check you."

"They may, but they don't usually look in the place where I plan to hide the mike."

"The tape's going to hurt coming off."

He laughed. "I'll give you the pleasure of removing it. You can comfort me afterward."

"You're liable to need a bandage."

"But your hands are so soothing."

"Thanks," she said, but she laughed, too, even though he was purposely trying to embarrass her, and Phyllis was watching. What the hell, she was in love.

And she was about to embark on a very dangerous mission.

During the drive to the warehouse where they were supposed to meet the caller, Kyle tried to reassure Laura by talking nonstop about anything and everything. "Tell me about your brothers," he said when he'd started the car.

"What about them?"

"Do they look like you?"

"No. They're all dark like my dad."

"Do you think they'll like me?"

"Are you intending to meet them?" she asked, surprised. "I thought you were going to give me some time to get accustomed to our relationship."

"I am. But in the meantime I thought I'd cover all the bases, and it won't hurt to enlist your family in my cause."

"Which is?"

"I told you this morning, to marry you," he answered simply. "So, do you think they'll like me?"

She laughed. "Believe me, you're enough of a male chauvinist that I imagine you'll get along fine."

"What about your mother? Does she like male chauvinists?"

"She likes my father." Laura glanced at the walkie-talkie lying on the seat beside them, only then remembering that everyone else had one, too, and that theirs was tuned to the microphones she and Kyle were wearing. Obviously the entire team had overheard their conversation. Had Kyle known? "By the way, I meant to tell you that I adore your teddy bear."

"What?" Kyle frowned at her.

"Your teddy bear."

"What are you talking about, Laura?"

She spoke directly into the microphone. "Doesn't everybody know that you sleep with a teddy bear? I'm sorry, Kyle. I didn't mean to embarrass you, but Smoky's so cute."

"Kyle's cute," a male voice broke in on the walkie-talkie. Stan? Or Jim, maybe. "The boys downtown are going to love that, boss. Say, what color is Smoky?"

"Pink," Kyle answered, sneering at Laura. "With blue eyes."

"Sounds good."

They joked around for the rest of the ride, until Kyle pulled in front of the warehouse. "This is serious business now, folks," he remarked. "Heads up."

The transition was instant. Looking at the dark, abandoned building, Laura felt her heart start to pound with anticipation and dread. This *was* serious business. Danger lurked in that warehouse. Belying any anxiety at all, Kyle got out of the car and, taking her hand, walked beside her toward the structure. Since they were posing as husband and wife the gesture wouldn't seem out of place, but she was grateful for his support, no matter how casually it was offered.

"If anyone meets us, just take my cue," he said.

Laura nodded. "Okay."

"We're going to be suspicious ourselves."

"Right."

He opened the door and stepped into the darkness. Although he couldn't use police procedure—weapons drawn, crouching and entering warily—and maintain their ruse in case someone was watching, she could tell he was on alert. Every muscle was coiled for instant action.

"Stop right there," a low voice called.

Kyle froze with Laura behind him. "Who are you?" he asked. "Where are you? Look, buddy, I don't like to deal with ghosts."

All of a sudden light flooded the building. The pawnbroker from the day before stepped in front of them. He glanced at Laura. "How's your ring, honey?"

"Fine," she answered. "Very nice."

The man turned back to Kyle. "Let's see your chest."

"For what? You like chests?"

"I don't like cops. And cops wear wires." When Kyle had pulled open his shirt the man nodded. "How about the little lady?"

"Sorry. The little lady isn't going to open her shirt for you, buddy."

"Too bad." But the man smiled and held out a briefcase he was carrying. "Okay, we deal anyhow. Look, I got something special for you."

"Oh, yeah?" Kyle pretended he wasn't convinced. "You alone?"

"What's it matter?"

"You don't like cops. I don't like cruds. I may be from another country, but I know enough to keep my back protected."

"I'm alone."

Again Kyle didn't look convinced. "What is it you've got?"

"An Uzi."

"So?"

"So it's one hell of a weapon."

"What good is one gun?" Kyle asked.

"It's better than none," the man answered. "I thought you had a cause."

Kyle glared at him. "My cause needs more than a single Israeli-design submachine gun."

"Could be there's more where that came from." The man shrugged. "I don't know. I gotta see."

"See who? Who's your source?"

The man laughed and shook his head. "I told you, I work alone. I deal alone. I just run a pawnshop and buy little gee-gaws that people can't use no more. I don't got no sources."

"Sure."

"Look, man, you and your people gotta learn to be patient. This is America. We do things differently."

Kyle practically sneered. "We don't have time for patience. My people put the word out on the streets yesterday. We need guns and we need them fast. Now are you gonna produce, or are you wasting my time?"

"Tell you what, I got one gun for you. Cheap. You take it or you lose it."

"I'll take it," Kyle said. "You got it with you?"

The man flipped open his briefcase. An Uzi sat nestled inside. "You got the cash?"

"Of course." Kyle glanced at Laura. "Give the man some money, babe."

Laura had been watching the interchange with more than typical interest. For some reason she didn't believe that this man was alone, either, but that wouldn't be unusual. Kyle had kept their backs to the wall, so there was no reason to think someone would be able to sneak up on them. So why was she so wary? Then, as the man reached out his pudgy hand for the money, she realized what bothered her about him. He'd been part of Tony Calimara's organization, she remembered now. She'd seen his name on files—it was Vito Morgan. Panic welled inside Laura like a storm, and she stood there staring at him, the thought of dealing with anyone connected with Tony Calimara paralyzing her.

"Hey, babe?" Kyle said. "What's wrong?"

"Maybe she don't want to let loose of the purse strings," Vito joked.

To her distress Laura realized her hands were trembling. "I—"

"Give the man the money, babe," Kyle said again, but Laura didn't move. She couldn't. Finally he reached in her purse and pulled out several hundred dollar bills. "How much?"

"What'd I do to scare you, honey?" Vito asked, staring at Laura.

"How much do you want for the gun?" Kyle asked.

"Five bills." Vito kept frowning at Laura.

Kyle peeled off the money and took the briefcase. Placing his arm around Laura's shoulders he said, "You'll have to pardon my wife. She's been kind of spooky lately. She's pregnant, and guns bother her."

"And you're looking for a ton of them?"

"Even though they bother her we don't want to raise a kid in this world. We're gonna fix it first. Look, anything else comes into the pawnshop, you call. Hear?"

"Sure thing."

Before the man could ask anything else, Kyle guided Laura out of the building and into the car. After he had started it and pulled out onto the street he sighed with relief. "We're clear," he said for the benefit of the people monitoring them. "Meet at the Federal Building.

Shut down on the communications. Clear the channel."
When the static from their walkie-talkie stopped, indicating that everything had been shut down and no one was listening, he glanced at her. "What the hell was that all about, Laura?"

"I froze," she said, at last. She was trembling so badly now that she could hardly speak.

"Yes, but the question is, why?"

"God, Kyle, I'm sorry."

"Tell me what happened, Laura," he said firmly.

"I recognized him. Vito Morgan. He's part of Tony Calimara's organization."

As though realizing what terror that knowledge had struck in her heart, Kyle covered her hand with his own. "Tony Calimara's in jail, Laura. He can't hurt you."

"I know," she answered. "Oh, God, Kyle, I'm sorry."

"It's okay."

"No, it's not okay. I froze back there, and I could have gotten us both killed. I could have blown this whole operation."

"But you didn't."

"Only because you were there," she said. "Look, I've asked you to transfer me; you can't keep me now. Obviously I'm not ready."

"I think you are, Laura."

She stared at him in disbelief. "How long are you going to keep covering up for me, Kyle, and backing me up? What does it take to convince you that I can't deal with the streets anymore? Hell, for that matter, what does it take to convince me? Why did I ever apply for this job? I could have stayed on the beat—"

"That's enough, Laura. You froze and it's over. Forget it, now. We've got to prepare for the rest of this operation."

"Count me out."

"I'm counting you in, and I don't want to hear any more objections," he said in no uncertain terms. "I'm in charge here." It surprised Laura that he was pulling rank, but he certainly could do so. He was in charge.

For the rest of the ride they spoke little. When they arrived at the Federal Building, Kyle pulled into the same dark garage they'd used before and turned to her. "I have faith in you, Laura."

She sighed. "You know, I believe the philosophers are right: Love is blind."

He smiled. "Maybe, but love doesn't have a thing to do with my decision. I truly believe that it was the thought of Calimara that upset you."

"What if I see him, Kyle?" she asked. "How would I react then?"

He covered her hand again in a gesture of support. "Don't worry, Laura. You won't see him. Like I said, Tony Calimara is in jail. And now that you've realized who Vito Morgan is, you can deal with him, too. I'm sure of it. And if you need further evidence of your ability, I'll take you back to the shooting range and you can show off."

"That won't be necessary," she said, her confidence growing again. Maybe Kyle was right, her reaction was to the thought of Calimara, and now that she knew that, she could deal with it. "Thanks anyway."

"No problem. Laura—" Touching her chin with his finger, he turned her to face him. "Unfortunately I will have to transfer you if you freeze up again."

She nodded. "I know. And I understand."

"By the way," he went on in a joking manner, the

incident already forgotten, "better get your hands ready. I've got a lot of tape that needs to be removed."

Vito Morgan didn't call again that day. Or the day after. The entire team was growing impatient, but they worked the streets as usual, pretending to be looking for an arsenal of weapons. They had certainly been buying and word was out on the street. In addition to every kind of gun imaginable, Kyle had bought a case of hand grenades just yesterday from a man who had approached them in a restaurant while they were eating, and the day before he had gotten a Laws rocket from a pimply-faced teenager. Where the kid had gotten hold of such a destructive weapon remained unanswered, but they consoled themselves with the knowledge that, while he was getting off scot-free, he didn't have any more weapons, or he would have tried to sell them, too.

In the end, they had to remember that the guns they were collecting by accident were penny-ante in comparison to the big bust they were working on. At least they got the weapons off the street.

"I realize this is part of the job, but it's really disappointing to keep coming up empty-handed," Laura remarked as they went out the door of another musty pawnshop. It was a hot spring afternoon. Birds sang in leafy trees, flowers bloomed in empty lots, all belying the dirt and squalor of the neighborhood. "Maybe whoever stole those Uzis has taken them somewhere else to sell."

"They're here." Kyle sidestepped an overflowing garbage can. "We've found another one."

"When?" Laura was surprised. They'd been together every moment since the night he'd made love to her on board his boat.

"Late last night. Accidentally. As I understand it, a blue and white happened to stop a suspicious vehicle on the Kennedy Expressway and found it in the trunk."

"Same shipment?"

He nodded. "I checked the serial number. That makes four of them."

"How'd you hear?"

"Captain Warner called this morning when you were in the shower. He also told me he heard from a friend on the NYPD, and another shipment is missing from the docks."

The problem was escalating. Laura shook her head in frustration. "What can we do?"

"Keep looking. Something's bound to break soon. We've certainly been spreading enough cash around." He sighed. "You know, I think when we get done here I'd like to go after that kid who sold us that Laws rocket."

"He was quite a businessman, wasn't he?"

"It's a shame to think that there's a boy out there with that much chutzpah, and that it's misdirected. By the way, how's Kevin?"

"Still punished." They had stopped by her apartment for a few minutes last night to get her mail. Kyle had waited in the car. When Laura had managed to navigate through the maze of fake snakes and spider webs in the vestibule, a la *Raiders of the Lost Ark,* Kevin had giggled and come to the window and talked to her.

"The goldfish or Attila?"

"I don't think his mother knows about Attila yet."

"Did you give him the can of slime you bought?"

They hadn't used the stuff; they hadn't had to. "Yes. He loved it."

"Do you want a boy or a girl first?"

She smiled. She still hadn't given him her answer. "I want to catch a criminal first."

"Fair enough." He shrugged as they passed an ice-cream vendor. "How's Cassie?"

"Great. She liked you." They'd gone out to dinner last night, and Laura had met the construction worker, who seemed to have fallen hard for her friend.

"I liked her, too. She's rather frank."

"Rather." All during dinner Cassie had raved on about obelisks and phallic symbols. She'd just discovered that the Washington Monument was built in that tradition, and she had been furious.

Kyle paused by the vendor. "How about a Popsicle? We could use a break."

"Sounds good."

They stood near the curb eating and enjoying the spring day. As usual, he watched her. By now Laura was well aware of his fetish with her mouth, and sometimes she ignored his seething glances and sometimes she didn't. At the moment, she was feeling devilish and she smiled as she slid her lips sensuously over the cold, frozen creation.

"Laura, don't do that," he said, hitching his breath in harshly.

"Why not?"

"You know it drives me crazy."

"You need to learn tolerance, Kyle. I hear it's good for the soul."

"But hell on the body. You're getting to be a regular tease, Laura."

With a husky laugh, she wiped a drip of Popsicle from his hand with one finger and brought it to her mouth, rubbing it slowly across her lips.

"Damn," he sucked his breath in again. "Wait until I get you home."

She laughed again but the laughter died in her throat as a shadow fell across her face. Looking up, she stared at the face of the pawnbroker.

"Still looking for weapons?" Vito Morgan asked in a low, secretive tone.

"We sure are," Kyle said. "What have you got?"

"A shipment of Uzis."

"Where?"

"On, no, I'm not gonna tell you where."

"When, then?"

"One hundred grand."

"Don't worry, we've got the money," Kyle said.

"Maybe I ought to ask who your source is," Morgan answered sleazily. "You been throwing a lot of money around."

"Didn't you know? Causes are always well funded."

Vito didn't press further. "Fifteen minutes," he said. "Same warehouse. Just the two of you."

"I can't get the money in fifteen minutes," Kyle said.

"Why not? You live close by, don't you? Thirty minutes, or no deal." With that he turned and hurried away.

Both Laura and Kyle stared after him. "This is it," Kyle said moments later, tossing what remained of the ice cream in the trash. "Let's go. We don't have time to get wired. All we can do is contact everyone and get set up."

Earlier, they had managed to get blueprints of the inside of the warehouse and had developed a contingency plan just in case something like this happened. Phyllis and Sam were to position themselves just outside the west entrance and Stan and Jim the east side. The arrest would be made when the contacts left the building with the money, which Kyle had checked out of Evidence and kept in a nearby locker.

They headed for the bus station. Laura was really nervous. She stood by anxiously as Kyle opened the locker with a key and took out the briefcase carrying several hundred thousand dollars in marked one-hundred-dollar bills. If they lost this money, whether by theft or by carelessness, they would be in deep, deep trouble with Internal Affairs. The derelicts hanging around the bus station had made her nervous; she'd been certain they'd break into the locker and take the money. But it was still there.

Kyle pulled it out, and they went back to the car. "Check your gun," he instructed. Laura took out her weapon and clicked it off safety, tucking it in the folds of her skirt. Thank goodness she was wearing one today. Considering the reputation of Vito Morgan, she wasn't going to take any chances and leave the darned gun in her purse.

"Ready?" Kyle asked as they pulled in front of the warehouse with five minutes to spare.

Since they knew the locations of the rest of the team, they didn't have to look around to know that the others had arrived, too. The question was had Vito Morgan come?

"Ready," Laura answered as the overhead door opened, and they drove the car inside. The darkness of the warehouse was just as frightening as before. Laura's heart thudded as they got out of the car.

"Anybody here?" Kyle called.

"Hold up," the voice of Vito Morgan stopped them. "You got the money?"

Kyle held up the briefcase. "You got the goods?"

"Right here." He gestured to several wooden cases

sitting on a pallet. "Send the little lady upstairs with the money."

"We'll both go upstairs with the money," Kyle said.

"Nope," Morgan insisted. "She goes alone. You get to help me load."

"What's the matter," Kyle asked, "don't you trust me?"

"Don't feel bad, man, I don't trust my own mother. If we deal, it's my way or nothing at all. I load these machine guns, and you could drive right out of here without paying me. She goes alone."

"I don't like it," Kyle muttered to Laura. "Something stinks. Something's wrong."

"Nothing's wrong," Laura answered. "Morgan's just being cautious."

"I don't like it," Kyle said again.

"Everything will work out fine." She took the briefcase from him and stepped forward.

"Laura—"

"Where to?" she called to Morgan.

"Up the steps and to your right. The banker will be waiting."

"Look, buddy," Kyle warned, "anything happens to her and you'll answer to me."

"Calm down, mister. Nothing's gonna happen to sweetie pie. She's just gonna make the payment, and she'll meet you back down here in a flash. I'll be one-hundred grand richer, and you'll be the owners of several hundred Uzis."

Now that her eyes had adjusted to the darkness Laura could see much better. Not that it helped. She didn't trust Vito Morgan one single bit and as she went up the steps to the room at the top, she stayed on alert.

She could hear Kyle and Morgan loading the guns.

In the distance she heard a siren. Vito Morgan heard it, too. It had to be the intensity of the situation that caused him to react to it so violently. Suddenly he turned and swore at Kyle. "Damn you. This is a double cross, isn't it?"

"What the hell?" Kyle ducked as Morgan drew a gun and fired. "Laura!"

Laura had arrived at the room. She had been about to open the door when the gunshots echoed through the warehouse, ricocheting off the walls. At the same moment a man opened the door to the room and stepped out to see about the ruckus. Obviously it was too late to keep up the ruse. "Police," she said, dropping the briefcase and cocking her own weapon. "Freeze."

The man turned to her and Laura saw that he was tall, thin, well dressed with dark, slightly graying hair. "Well, hello, Laura," he said. "Fancy meeting you here."

Tony Calimara looked exactly the same as he had eight months ago: arrogant, sleazy, and overbearing. "Calimara," she breathed as her heart hit the floor in terror. "What are you doing out of jail?"

He smiled. "I'm out on a technicality. Didn't anyone notify you?"

Since Kyle had kept the captain posted of their progress, she hadn't had to check in, and had obviously missed the notification.

"You people should learn to do things right."

"We didn't make any mistakes."

"The judge seemed to think so. And you're making another mistake now." He nodded at her weapon and at Kyle, who was holding a gun on Morgan. "Call off the dogs."

"No," she said.

"You won't arrest me, Laura," he answered. "You can't."

She felt her stomach start to churn at the sound of his soft, wheedling voice. "Yes, I can."

"Come now, love, you couldn't even press charges against me the last time, not that I did anything to you that you didn't want."

"Crud," Kyle swore from below. "You lousy crud."

In the distance they could hear more sirens. This time, they were coming to the warehouse for certain. The rest of the team burst through the doors, but Calimara stood in front of Laura, still smiling arrogantly. "I'm going to walk out of here, Laura, and you're going to let me."

She heard Kyle move to the steps. Apparently Phyllis had taken over for him. "Laura?"

She glanced at him from the corner of her eye. "I'm fine, Kyle."

"Move away, Laura," he said, and she knew he was planning to shoot. Obviously he thought she had frozen again.

She shook her head. Kyle was right. All she needed was the confidence of one arrest, this one. "No. I can do this. I can manage."

"Laura, move."

Calimara smiled. "Don't want your lover killed, eh, Laura?" he said. "I must have been pretty good."

She ignored his taunt and she ignored Kyle. This was between her and Tony Calimara. "You were awful," she answered him softly, "and if nothing else I will get you for rape. I'll press charges." She had finally figured out her problem. All these months she had blamed herself for what he had done to her. She'd thought she was at fault because she was a cop and had put herself in the position of being raped. "I intend to prosecute you to the fullest, Mr. Calimara."

"It'll never stick. I'll get out."

"We'll see. In the meantime we have a weapons charge here that looks pretty ironclad. This will put you away for ten years at least. Turn around and put your hands on the wall," she said, aiming her weapon straight at his forehead. "You're under arrest."

"You won't do this, Laura."

"Watch me." She cocked the weapon. "Turn around. Spread eagle!" When he turned around, she quickly frisked him and then stepped back. "You have the right to remain silent—"

"If you give up that right," Stan broke in, walking up the steps and taking over, "whatever you say can be used against you in a court of law."

Stan's voice droned on, but Laura didn't listen. She turned around to glance at Kyle, who was smiling at her. "Good job."

"Oh, God, I was scared," she said. She felt like laughing and crying at the same time. "I was so scared." She fell into his arms. "Do we have them?"

"Dead to rights."

"They didn't take the money."

"But they had the guns. I'll bet anything if we check the records in that office we'll find out that Calimara owns this warehouse."

"Will it be enough?"

"Combined with the other charges—whatever he got out on—it'll be plenty. I was really proud of you, Laura."

She smiled. "Thank you, Kyle. Thank you for giving me this chance, and for being at my side."

"I'm willing to be at your side forever, Laura. You

know that. All you have to say is the word."

"Come on, Laura," Stan said. The team stood around them in a circle, smiling. The police were taking Tony and Vito away in a squad car. "Make the man happy."

"Why not?" she said. "I've always wanted to get married and have a pack of kids." And she was whole now, even stronger than before. "By the way, I want at least five of them."

Kyle frowned. "Kids?"

"Teddy bears."

He laughed, grabbing her and kissing her right there, in front of everyone. "Come on, Laura," he said, "let's go take off some tape."

"You don't have any tape on."

"Minor detail. We'll stop and buy some." He put his arm around her. "I need to get a roller-skate key, anyhow."

"Why?"

"A long time ago you told me you liked to roller-skate. I want to have the key."

She laughed and leaned her head on his shoulder. "Kyle Patterson, my family is going to love you."

"It's your love I'm interested in."

"And that," she said, "you've already got. Forever."

EPILOGUE

KYLE DROPPED THE ANCHOR and turned to watch the sunset with Laura. She sat in the same seat she had occupied so many months ago, when he'd first brought her on board the *Water Witch*, but she wasn't afraid anymore, although she wore the silly orange life-jacket. It looked so odd on her, sticking out over her slightly protruding abdomen. He went to her and sat behind her, sliding his hand around her waist.

"Is Junior kicking?" he asked.

She turned to him and as always, her smile took his breath away. "Yes. He's being a devil tonight, but I thought we'd agreed his name was going to be Kevin."

Not many people decided to name their child after a five-year-old, but after exhausting the name book, they had settled on Kevin because that child had been so instrumental in their relationship. "We might have a girl. Don't you think we should consider a few female names?"

Laura shook her head firmly. "He's a boy."

Kyle laughed. "How can you be so sure?"

"A mother knows these things."

He laughed again. "Sure. Whatever you say, Mom. Come here and snuggle."

She did, nestling her head against his shoulder as she toyed with the thick gold band on her finger. "You know, I think I could stay out here forever, on the water, watching the sky."

"Forever is a long time," Kyle remarked.

"Mmm," she agreed. "A long time."

"Feeling okay?"

"Fine. I like being pregnant."

"I like you," he answered, rubbing his hand gently over her abdomen.

She leaned her head back so that she could see him. "Want to go below?"

"For what?"

"Oh, I don't know," she teased, "I could show you my stretch marks and you could show me your gun."

He laughed. "Shame on you, Laura. You have a nasty mind."

"And a healthy appetite."

"I think I've created a monster," he said, pulling her closer. God, he loved this woman. He wanted to be with her always, to walk beside her and love her.

Actually, though, he was glad she could joke, particularly about sex. The past six months had been difficult for both of them. They had gotten married, then she became pregnant, but the trial had taken all their energies. Following through on her threat, she had prosecuted Tony Calimara for rape. It had been hell to stand beside her, to take her hand, to touch her during the proceedings without rushing up to strangle the mobster.

Yet she was right. Tony Calimara could never touch her again, physically or emotionally. She'd stood up to him and she'd won. She'd put him away for a long, long time. Even if he got out of jail on a technicality for one charge, there was always the next charge, the conviction for weapons. And they'd gotten an additional sentence for drug dealing.

The whole mess was finally over, and they were putting their lives together at last. "What did Captain Warner say about your leave of absence?" he asked.

"Not to be gone too long." She smiled. "Don't you want to go below?"

"Actually, the prospect of seeing your stretch marks is very tempting, but I thought you wanted to watch the sunset."

"The sun has set. Oh—" She squirmed around in his arms so that she could see him. "Speaking of Captain Warner, I forgot to tell you. When I went in today, Jim Hines had a detail for me. He's investigating a doctor suspected of doing some big time drugs. Do you believe he wanted me to pose as a dealer?"

"Pregnant?"

"Yes. He thought it would be a perfect cover."

"Is the doctor an obstetrician?"

"No, just a regular doctor."

"I'm glad you turned it down." Kyle paused. "You did turn it down?"

"Yes, I'm afraid I'm not up to quick-drawing dressed in maternity clothes." All of a sudden she traced her finger along his lips. "Thank you, Kyle, for making me whole again."

His heartbeat quickened. "Thank you, Laura, for coming into my life," he answered, "and for letting me be the other half of the whole."

She smiled. "This sounds like a mutual admiration society."

"Close," he said. "Although you don't appreciate me the way you should."

She laughed again. "Did I ever tell you that you're a chauvinist?"

"All the time."

She sighed. "Kyle? What are we going to do with all the people who are coming to visit?"

In addition to his sister, they had discovered that her parents and all of her brothers were planning to visit after the baby's birth. They'd come for the wedding and had had such a great time that they all wanted to come back. He shrugged. "The apartment?"

"I suppose. We could stay on the boat."

"If it gets crowded, we could house them at the Wilson Arms."

She laughed. "Oh, sure, they'd love that."

"Your brothers would be delighted. I keep telling you they don't get much action in Kansas City."

"Kyle, Kansas City is not a cow town," she said.

"And you're not a country girl?"

"No, I'm not."

"You're right," he said, nuzzling her neck with his lips. "You're my girl, and I love you."

She melted in his arms. "I love you," she answered. The night fell, surrounding them, shrouding them as the boat bobbed up and down in the water. "I feel it," she murmured.

"What?"

"The magic."

Kyle looked out over the hill at the city lights in the distance. Other boats bobbed white on the horizon. "So do I," he answered, taking her into his arms and kissing her. "God, so do I. Let's go below," he suggested this time.

"For what?"

He gazed deeply into her eyes, letting her see the love in his heart. "More magic."

SECOND CHANCE AT LOVE

___ 0-425-10048-0	**IN NAME ONLY** #400 Mary Modean	$2.25
___ 0-425-10049-9	**RECLAIM THE DREAM** #401 Liz Grady	$2.25
___ 0-425-10050-2	**CAROLINA MOON** #402 Joan Darling	$2.25
___ 0-425-10051-0	**THE WEDDING BELLE** #403 Diana Morgan	$2.25
___ 0-425-10052-9	**COURTING TROUBLE** #404 Laine Allen	$2.25
___ 0-425-10053-7	**EVERYBODY'S HERO** #405 Jan Mathews	$2.25
___ 0-425-10080-4	**CONSPIRACY OF HEARTS** #406 Pat Dalton	$2.25
___ 0-425-10081-2	**HEAT WAVE** #407 Lee Williams	$2.25
___ 0-425-10082-0	**TEMPORARY ANGEL** #408 Courtney Ryan	$2.25
___ 0-425-10083-9	**HERO AT LARGE** #409 Steffie Hall	$2.25
___ 0-425-10084-7	**CHASING RAINBOWS** #410 Carole Buck	$2.25
___ 0-425-10085-5	**PRIMITIVE GLORY** #411 Cass McAndrew	$2.25
___ 0-425-10225-4	**TWO'S COMPANY** #412 Sherryl Woods	$2.25
___ 0-425-10226-2	**WINTER FLAME** #413 Kelly Adams	$2.25
___ 0-425-10227-0	**A SWEET TALKIN' MAN** #414 Jackie Leigh	$2.25
___ 0-425-10228-9	**TOUCH OF MIDNIGHT** #415 Kerry Price	$2.25
___ 0-425-10229-7	**HART'S DESIRE** #416 Linda Raye	$2.25
___ 0-425-10230-0	**A FAMILY AFFAIR** #417 Cindy Victor	$2.25
___ 0-425-10513-X	**CUPID'S CAMPAIGN** #418 Kate Gilbert	$2.50
___ 0-425-10514-8	**GAMBLER'S LADY** #419 Cait Logan	$2.50
___ 0-425-10515-6	**ACCENT ON DESIRE** #420 Christa Merlin	$2.50
___ 0-425-10516-4	**YOUNG AT HEART** #421 Jackie Leigh	$2.50
___ 0-425-10517-2	**STRANGER FROM THE PAST** #422 Jan Mathews	$2.50
___ 0-425-10518-0	**HEAVEN SENT** #423 Jamisan Whitney	$2.50
___ 0-425-10530-X	**ALL THAT JAZZ** #424 Carole Buck	$2.50
___ 0-425-10531-8	**IT STARTED WITH A KISS** #425 Kit Windham	$2.50
___ 0-425-10558-X	**ONE FROM THE HEART** #426 Cinda Richards	$2.50
___ 0-425-10559-8	**NIGHTS IN SHINING SPLENDOR** #427 Christina Dair	$2.50
___ 0-425-10560-1	**ANGEL ON MY SHOULDER** #428 Jackie Leigh	$2.50
___ 0-425-10561-X	**RULES OF THE HEART** #429 Samantha Quinn	$2.50
___ 0-425-10604-7	**PRINCE CHARMING REPLIES** #430 Sherryl Woods	$2.50
___ 0-425-10605-5	**DESIRE'S DESTINY** #431 Jamisan Whitney	$2.50
___ 0-425-10680-2	**A LADY'S CHOICE** #432 Cait Logan	$2.50
___ 0-425-10681-0	**CLOSE SCRUTINY** #433 Pat Dalton	$2.50
___ 0-425-10682-9	**SURRENDER THE DAWN** #434 Jan Mathews	$2.50
___ 0-425-10683-7	**A WARM DECEMBER** #435 Jacqueline Topaz	$2.50
___ 0-425-10708-6	**RAINBOW'S END** #436 Carole Buck (On sale Apr. '88)	$2.50
___ 0-425-10709-4	**TEMPTRESS** #437 Linda Raye (On sale Apr. '88)	$2.50